"Are you Gaia?"

"Uh, yeah." Gaia was surprised on two counts. The first was that the girl knew her name at all; the second was that she actually pronounced it right on the first try.

"I'm Cassie," said the girl. "Cassie Greenman."

How wonderful for you, thought Gaia. She had noticed the girl in class before. Although she hadn't seen her running with the core popular-people crowd, Gaia assumed that Cassie was in on the anti-Gaia coalition.

"Aren't you worried?" Cassie asked.

"What am I supposed to be worried about?" Gaia wondered if she had missed the announcement of a history exam or some similar nonevent. Or maybe this girl was talking about Gaia's upcoming date. Maybe Heather and pals really were planning some horrible heap of humiliation.

Not that Gaia cared.

The girl rolled her eyes. "About being next."

"The next what?" Gaia asked.

"You know." Cassie raised a hand to her throat and drew one silver-blue-painted fingernail across the pale skin of her throat. "Being the next one killed."

Don't miss any books in this thrilling series:

FEARLESS™

Available from SIMON PULSE

FEARLESS™

TWISTED

FRANCINE PASCAL

SIMON PULSE
New York   London   Toronto   Sydney   Singapore

To Johnny Stewart Carmen

First Simon Pulse printing July 2002

Text copyright © 2000 by Francine Pascal
Cover copyright © 2000 by 17th Street Productions,
an Alloy Inc. company

SIMON PULSE
An imprint of Simon & Schuster Children's Publishing Division
1230 Avenue of the Americas, New York, NY 10020

Produced by 17th Street Productions,
an Alloy, Inc. company
151 West 26th Street
New York, NY 10001

Printed in the United States of America
10 9 8 7 6 5 4

This book has been cataloged with the Library of Congress.
ISBN: 0-671-03944-X

TWISTED

There are circles in Hell.

My father—back when he still cared that I was alive and breathing—used to make me read. Not easy stuff. Even when I was a kid, there was no *Winnie-the-Pooh*, no *Little House on the Prairie*. Not for me.

It was all about the classics. *Hard* classics.

One of the moldy oldies he put under my nose was *The Inferno*, by Dante. This book was seriously tough sledding. The whole thing was written in verse, and it was full of political stuff that didn't always make a lot of sense, and the language was creaky to say the least. But there were good parts.

In this story a guy gets led all around Hell to see how everybody is punished. A lot of it is kind of like you would expect. Lots of demons with whips. Fire. Snakes. That kind of thing.

But the idea that stuck with me was the way Hell was divided

up in circles. The dead guys up
in the first circle don't have it
so bad. It's just kind of rainy
and dull up there. But the really
bad people, like murderers (or
members of a political party
Dante didn't like), they get
shoved way down to a circle where
they have to run around without
feet or burst into flame or get
eaten by big lizards or melt like
candles.

I remembered this book the
other day and started thinking
that my life could be sliced up
in the same way as hell.

There are the little things.
Finding out the deli is out of
Krispy Kreme. Losing a chess game
against some moron I should have
schooled. That's the gloomy,
first-circle sort of hell.

Then there's having to live
with George and Ella. George knew
my father, but I don't really
know him. Ella didn't know my
father, doesn't know me, and I
don't even *want* to know Ella.

She's definitely a deeper level
of hell.

The next level down is high
school. It gets a level of hell
all to itself.

Below that comes Sam and
Heather. I wouldn't throw Sam in
a pit by himself. I mean, Sam's
the guy I want to be with. The
only guy I've ever wanted to be
with. But Sam is with Heather,
and together they deserve pitch-
forks and brimstone.

Then there's my father. My
father disappears, doesn't write,
doesn't call, and doesn't give me
a clue about what's going on. Now
we're getting really deep. Snakes
and fire. Demons with weird Latin
names.

And my mom. The way I feel when
I think about her. When I think
about her death. Well, that brings
us right down to the bottom.

The way Dante tells it, the
very bottom layer of hell isn't
hot. Instead it's a big lake of
ice with people frozen inside.

They're stuck forever with only
their faces sticking out, and
every time they cry, it just adds
another layer of frost covering
their eyes.

Put my whole life together,
and that's where I am. Down on
the ice. Some days I feel like I
have a pair of skates. Other days
I wonder if Dante didn't get it
wrong. Maybe the ice isn't the
lowest level after all.

Her big pal gave her a little love pat—enough to bounce her from the wall and back to his beefy hand.

the high school circle

PRETTY PEOPLE DO UGLY THINGS.

It was one of those laws of nature that Gaia had understood for years. If she ever started to forget that rule for a second, there al-

Jerkus High-schoolensis

ways seemed to be some good-looking asshole ready to remind her.

She stumbled up the steps and pushed her way inside The Village School with five minutes to spare before her first class. Actually early. Of course, her hair was still wet from the shower and her homework wasn't done, but being there—actually physically inside the building before the bell rang—was a new experience. For twelve whole seconds after that, she thought she might have an all right day.

Then she caught a glimpse of one of those things that absolutely defines the high school circle of hell.

Down at the end of the row of lockers, a tall, broadshouldered guy was smiling a very confident smile, wearing very popular-crowd clothes, and using a very big hand to pin a very much smaller girl up against the wall. There was an amused expression on Mr. Handsome's face.

Only the girl who was stuck between his hand and fifty years' worth of ugly green paint didn't look like she thought it was funny.

Gaia had noticed the big boy in a couple of her classes but hadn't bothered to file away his name. Tad, she thought, or maybe it was Chip. She knew it was something like that.

From the way girls in class talked, he was supposed to be cute. Gaia could sort of see it. Big blue eyes. Good skin. Six-five even without the air soles in his two-hundred-dollar sneakers. His lips were a little puffy, but then, some people liked that. It was the hair that really eliminated him from Gaia's list of guys worth looking at.

He wore that stuff in his hair. The stuff that looked like a combination of motor oil and maple syrup. The stuff that made it look like he hadn't washed his hair this side of tenth grade. "What's the rush, Darla?" the Chipster said. "I just want to know what he said to you."

The girl, Darla, shook her head. "He didn't . . ."

Her big pal gave her a little love pat—enough to bounce her from the wall and back to his beefy hand.

"Don't give me that," he said, still all smiles. "I saw you two together."

Gaia did a quick survey of the hall. There was a trio of khaki-crowd girls fifty yards down and two leather dudes hanging near the front door. A skinny guy stuck his head out of a classroom, saw who was doing the shoving, and quickly ducked back in. Gaia

7

had to give him some credit. At least he looked. Everybody else in the hallway was Not Noticing so hard, it hurt.

Gaia really didn't need this. She didn't know the girl against the wall. Sure, the guy with the big hands was a prime example of Jerkus highschoolensis, but it was absolutely none of Gaia's business. She turned away and headed for class, wondering if she might avoid a tardy slip for the first time in a week.

"Just let me . . . ," the girl begged from behind her.

"In a minute, babe," replied the guy with the hands. "I just need to talk to you a little." There was a thump and a short whimper from the girl.

Gaia stopped. She really, really didn't need this.

She took a deep breath, turned, and headed back toward the couple.

The easiest thing would be to grab the guy by the face and teach him how soft a skull was compared to a concrete wall. But then, smashing someone's head would probably not help Gaia's reputation.

Words were an option. She hadn't used that method much, but there was a first time for everything, right?

She could try talking to the guy or even threatening to tell a teacher. Gaia didn't care if anyone at the school thought she was a wimp or a narc, or whatever they called it in New York City. That was the least of her problems. Besides, they already thought she was a bitch for not warning Heather about the park slasher.

Before long, Gaia was so close that both partners in the ugly little dance turned to look at her. Tough Guy's smile didn't budge an inch.

"What?" he said.

Gaia struggled for something to say. Something smooth. Something that would defuse this whole thing. She paused for a second, cleared her throat, and said . . .

"Is there . . . uh, some kind of a problem?"

Brilliant.

The guy who might be named Chip took a two-second look at her face, then spent twice as long trying to size up the breasts under Gaia's rumpled football shirt.

"Nothing you gotta worry about," he said, still staring at her chest. He waved the hand that wasn't busy holding a person. "This is a private conversation."

The girl against the wall looked at Gaia with a big-eyed, round-mouthed expression that could have been fear or hope or stupidity. Gaia's instant impression was that it was a little bit of all three. The girl had straight black hair that was turned up in a little flip, tanned-to-a-golden-brown skin, an excess of eye shadow, and a cheerleading uniform. She didn't exactly strike Gaia as a brain trust.

Not that being a cheerleader automatically made somebody stupid. Gaia was certain there were smart cheerleaders. Somewhere there had to be cheerleaders who were working on physics theories every time they put down their pom-poms. She hadn't met any, but they were out there. Probably living in the same city with all the nice guys who don't mind if a girl has thunder thighs and doesn't know how to dress.

"Well?" demanded Puffy Lips. "What's wrong with you? Are you deaf or just stupid?"

Gaia tensed. Anger left an acid taste in her throat. Suddenly her fist was crying out for his face. She opened her mouth to say something just as the bell for first period rang. So much for being on time.

She took a step closer to the pair. "Why don't you let her go?"

Chip made a little grunting laugh and shook his head. "Look, babe. Get out of here," he said to Gaia.

Babe. It wasn't necessarily an insult—unless the person saying it added that perfect tone of voice. The tone that says being a babe is on the same evolutionary rung as being a brain-damaged hamster.

Gaia glanced up the hallway. Only a few students were still in the hall, and none were close. If she planned to do anything without everyone in school seeing it, this was the time.

She leaned toward him. "Maybe *you'd* better get out of here," she said in a low voice. She could feel the cheerleader's short breaths on the back of her ne[...]. "You don't want to be late for class."

The sunny smile slipped from Chip's face, replaced by a go-away-you're-bothering-me frown. "Did you hear me tell you to go?"

Gaia shrugged. It was coming. That weird rush she sometimes felt.

"I heard you. I just didn't listen."

Now the expression on Chip's face was more like an I-guess-I'm-going-to-have-to-teach-you-how-the-world-works sneer. "Get the hell out of my way," he snapped.

"Make me."

He took his hand off Darla and grabbed Gaia by the arm.

Gaia was glad. If she touched him first, there was always the chance he would actually admit he got beat up by a girl and charge her with assault. But since Chip made the first move, all bets were off. Everything that happened from that first touch was self-defense.

Gaia was an expert in just about every martial art with a name. Jujitsu. Tai kwon do. Judo. Kung fu. If it involved hitting, kicking, or tossing people through the air, Gaia knew it. Standing six inches from Mr. Good Skin Bad Attitude, she could have managed a kick that would have taken his oily head right off his thick neck. She could have put a stiff hand through his rib cage or delivered a punch that drove his heart up against his spine.

11

But she didn't do any of that. She wanted to, but she didn't.

Moving quickly, she turned her arms and twisted out of his grip. Before Chip could react, she reached across with her left hand, took hold of the guy's right thumb, and gave it just a little . . . push.

For a moment Puffy Lips Chip looked surprised. Then Gaia pushed a little harder on his captive digit, and the look of surprise instantly turned to pain.

He tried to pull away, but Gaia held tight. She was working hard to keep from actually breaking his thumb. She could have broken his whole oversized hand like a bundle of big dry sticks. The real trick was hurting someone without really hurting someone. Don't break any bones. Don't leave any scars. Don't do anything permanent. Leave a memory.

"What do you think, Chip?" Gaia asked, still pushing his thumb toward the back of his hand. "Should you be shoving girls around?"

"Let go of me, you little—" He reached for her with his free hand.

Gaia leaned back out of his range and gave an extra shove. Chip wailed.

"Here's the deal," Gaia said quietly. "You keep your hands to yourself, I let you keep your hands. What do you think?"

Chip's knees were starting to shake, and there were beads of sweat breaking out on his forehead. "Who are—"

"Like I really want you to know my name." She pushed harder, and now Gaia could feel the bones in his thumb pulling loose from his hand. Another few seconds and one was sure to snap. "Do we have a deal?"

"Okay," he squeaked in a voice two octaves higher than it had been a few seconds before. "Sure."

Gaia let go. "That's good, Chip." The moment the physical conflict ended, Gaia felt all her uncertainty come rushing back. She glanced up the hallway and was relieved to see that there was no crowd of gawkers. That didn't stop her from feeling dizzy. She was acting like `muscle-bound freak girl` right in the main hallway at school. This was definitely not the way to remain invisible.

Puffy Lips stepped back and gripped his bruised thumb in his left hand. "Brad."

"What?"

"Brad," he said. "My name isn't Chip. It's Brad."

Gaia rolled her eyes. "Whatever." She lowered her head and shoved past him just as the late bell rang.

Another day, another fight, another tardy.

Things Gaia Knows

School sucks.

Ella sucks.

Her father sucks.

Heather Gannis sucks big time.

Things Gaia Wants to Know

Who kidnapped Sam?

Why did they contact her?

What was with all those stupid tests?

How could she have let the kidnappers get away after everything they'd done to her and Sam?

Why did Mr. Rupert use the words "all right" more often than most people used the word "the"?

Who killed CJ?

Why did she never know she had an uncle who looked exactly like her father?

Was said uncle going to contact her again?

Did she even want him to after he'd been nonexistent for her entire life?

Why did anyone in their right mind choose to drink skim milk?

Was she really expected to pay attention in class when there were things going on that actually mattered?

EVEN BACK WHEN HIS LEGS WORKED,

The Decision

Ed had never been fearless.

He sat in his first-period class and stared at the door. Any moment, the bell would ring. Then he would go out into the hallway and Gaia would appear. Any moment, he would have his chance. In the meantime he was terrified.

People who had seen him on a skateboard or a pair of in-lines might have been surprised to hear it. There had been no stairs too steep to slalom, no handrail Ed wasn't willing to challenge, no traffic too thick to dare. Anyone would tell you, Ed Fargo was a wild man. He took more risks, and took them faster, than any other boarder in the city.

The dark secret was that all through those days, almost every second, Ed had been terrified. Every time his wheels had sent sparks lancing from a metal rail, every time he had gone over a jump and felt gravity tugging down at his stomach, Ed had been sure he was about to die.

And when it didn't happen, when he landed, and lived, and rolled on to skate another day, it had been a thousand times sweeter just because he had been so scared. It seemed to Ed that there was nothing better than that moment after the terror had passed.

Then he lost the use of his legs and grew a wheelchair

15

on his butt, and everything changed. A wheelchair didn't give the sort of thrills you got from a skateboard. There were a few times, especially right after he realized he was never, ever going to get out of the chair, that Ed had thought about taking the contraption out into traffic—just to see how well it played with the taxis and delivery vans. That kind of thinking was scary in a whole different, definitely less fun way.

Legs or no legs, Ed wasn't sure that any stunt he had pulled in the past had terrified him as much as the one he was about to attempt.

He stared at the classroom door, and the blood rushing through his brain sounded as loud as a subway train pulling up to the platform.

He was going to tell Gaia Moore that he loved her.

He was really going to do it. If he didn't faint first.

Ed had been infatuated with Gaia since he first saw her in the school hallway. He was half smitten as soon as they spoke and all the way gone within a couple of days.

Since then, Ed and Gaia had become friends—or at least they had come as close to being friends as Gaia's don't-get-close-to-me forcefield would allow. To tell Gaia how he really felt would mean risking the relationship they already shared. Ed was horrified by the thought of losing contact with Gaia, but he was determined to take that chance.

For once, he was going to see what it was like to be fearless.

ONE IDIOT AN HOUR. GAIA FIGURED

Sour Seventeen

that if they would let her beat up one butthead per class, it would make the day go oh-so-smoothly. She would get the nervous energy out of her system, add a few high points to her dull-as-a-bowling-ball day, and by the time the final bell rang, the world would have eight fewer losers. All good things.

It might also help her keep her mind off Sam Moon. Sam, whose life she had saved more than once. Sam, who was oblivious to her existence. Sam, who had the biggest bitch this side of Fifth Avenue for a girlfriend but didn't seem to notice.

And still Gaia couldn't stop thinking about him. Daydreaming her way through each and every class. If her teachers had tested her on self-torture, she would have gotten an A.

Gaia trudged out of her third-period classroom and shouldered her way through the clogged hallway, her cruise control engaged. Every conscious brain cell was dedicated to the ongoing problem of what to do about her irritating and somewhat embarrassing Sam problem.

It was like a drug problem, only slightly less messy.

It was bad enough that Sam was with Heather. Even worse was Heather getting credit for everything Gaia did. Gaia had nearly lost her life saving Sam from a kidnapper. She had gone crazy looking for him. And then Heather had stepped in at the last second and looked like the big hero when her total expended effort was equal to drying her fingernails.

Not to mention the fact that the kidnappers had gotten away after they spent an entire day ordering her around as if she were a toy poodle.

Gaia suddenly realized she was biting her lip so badly that it was about to bleed. Whenever she thought about how the nameless, faceless men in black had used her, she got the uncontrollable urge to do serious violence to something. Then, of course, her thoughts turned directly to Heather.

And the fact that Heather had sex with Sam. And the fact that Heather had taken credit for saving Sam. And the fact that Heather got to hold hands with Sam and kiss Sam and talk to Sam and—

Gaia came to a stop in front of her locker and kicked it hard, denting the bottom of the door. A couple of Gap girls turned to stare, so Gaia kicked it again. The Gap girls scurried away.

She snarled at her vague reflection in the battered door. In the dull metal she was only an outline. That's all she was to Sam, too. A vague shadow of nothing much.

For a few delusional days Gaia had thought Sam might be the one. The one to break her embarrassing record as the only unkissed seventeen-year-old on planet Earth. Maybe even the one to turn sex from hypothesis into reality. But it wasn't going to happen.

There wasn't going to be any sex. There was never going to be any kissing. Not with Sam. Not ever.

Gaia yanked open the door of her locker, tossed in the book she was carrying, and randomly took out another without bothering to look at it. Then she slammed the door just as hard as she had kicked it.

She squeezed her eyes shut for a moment, squeezed hard, as if she could squeeze out her unwanted thoughts.

Even though Gaia knew zilch about love, knew less about relationships, and knew even less about psychology, she knew exactly what her girlfriends, if she had any, would tell her.

Find a new guy. Someone to distract you. Someone who cares about you.

Right. No problem.

Unfortunately, it had only taken her seventeen years to find a guy who didn't care about her.

NAVIGATION OF HIGH SCHOOL HALL-

ways takes on a whole new meaning when you're three feet wide and mounted on wheels.

Ed Fargo skidded around a corner, narrowly avoided a collision with a janitor, then spun right past a knot of students

The Attempt

laughing at some private joke. He threw the chair into hard reverse and did a quick 180 to dodge a stream of band students lugging instruments out a doorway, then he powered through a gap, coasted down a ramp, and took the next corner so hard, he went around on one wheel.

Fifty feet away, Gaia Moore was just shutting the door of her locker. Ed let the chair coast to a halt as he watched her. Gaia's football shirt was wrinkled, and her socks didn't match. Most of her yellow hair had slipped free of whatever she had been using to hold it in a ponytail. Loose strands hovered around the sculpted planes of her face, and the remaining hair gathered at the back of her head in a heavy, tumbled mass.

She was the most beautiful thing that Ed had ever seen.

He gave the wheels of his chair a sharp push and darted ahead of some slow walkers. Before Gaia could take two steps, Ed was at her side.

"Looking for your next victim?" he asked.

Gaia glanced down, and for a moment the characteristic frown on her insanely kissable lips was replaced by a smile. "Hey, Ed. What's up?"

Ed almost turned around and left. Why should he push it? He could live on that smile for at least a month.

Fearless, he told himself. Be fearless.

"I guess you don't want us to win at basketball this year," he started, trying to keep the tone light.

Gaia looked puzzled. "What?"

"The guy you went after this morning, Brad Reston," Ed continued. "He's a starting forward."

"How did you hear about it?" The frown was back full force.

"From Darla Rigazzi," Ed answered. "She's talked you up in every class this morning."

"Yeah, well, I wish she wouldn't." She looked away and started up the hallway again, the smooth muscles of her legs stretching under faded jeans.

Ed kept pace for fifty feet. Twice he opened his mouth to say something, but he shut it again before a word escaped. There was a distant, distracted look on Gaia's face now. The moment had passed. He would have to wait.

No, a voice said from the back of his mind. Don't wait. Tell her now. Tell her everything.

"Gaia . . . ," he started.

Something in his tone must have caught Gaia's attention. She stopped in the middle of one long stride and turned to him. Her right eyebrow was raised, and her changing eyes were the blue-gray of the Atlantic fifty miles off the coast. "What's wrong, Ed?"

Ed swallowed. Suddenly he felt like he was back on his skateboard, ready to challenge the bumpy ride down another flight of steps—only the steps in front of him went down, and down, and down forever.

He swallowed hard and shook his head. "It's not important."

I love you.

"Nothing at all, really."

I want to be with you.

"Just . . . nothing in particular."

I want you to be with me.

"I'll talk to you after class."

Gaia stared at him for a moment longer, then nodded. "All right. I'll see you later." She turned around and walked off quickly, her long legs eating up the distance.

"Perfect," Ed whispered to her retreating back.

A perfect pair. She was brave to the point of almost being dangerous, and he was gutless to the point of almost being depressing.

Sometimes I wonder what I would say if I were ever asked out on a date.

You'd think that since it's never happened to me, I might have had some time in the past seventeen years to formulate the perfect response. You'd think that with all the movies I've seen, I would have at least picked up some cheesy line. Some doe-eyed, swooning acceptance.

But I pretty much stay away from romantic comedies. There's no relationship advice to be had from a Neil LaBute film.

Besides, you can't formulate the perfect response for a situation you can't remotely imagine.

I figure that if it ever does happen (not probable), I'll end up saying something along the lines of "uh" or slight variations thereof.

"Uh . . . uh," if the guy's a freak.

"Uh . . . huh," if the guy's a nonfreak.

I wonder what Heather said to Sam when he first asked her out. Probably something disgustingly perfect. Something right out of a movie. Something like, "I was wondering when you'd ask." Or maybe Heather asked Sam out. And he said something like, "It would be my honor."

Okay. Stomach now reacting badly. Must think about something else.

What did Heather say when *Ed* asked her out?

Okay. Stomach now severely cramping.

So what happens after the "Uh . . . huh"?

Awkward pauses, I assume. Idiot small talk, sweaty palms (his), dry mouth (also his), bad food. (I imagine dates don't happen at places where they have good food—like Gray's Papaya or Dojo's.)

And I won't even get into what happens after the most likely difficult digestion. What does

the nonfreak expect at that
point? Hand holding? Kissing?
Groping? Heavy groping? Sex?

Stomach no longer wishes to be
a component of body.

Must stop here.

Luckily I won't ever have to
deal with any of this. Because no
nonfreak will ever ask me out.
And no freak will ever get more
than the initial grunt.

And with
those words,
Gaia's

painfully
seventeen-
beautiful

year streak
officially
came to an
end.

The Offer

THE SCHEDULE WAS A XEROX. Maybe a Xerox of a Xerox. Whatever it was, the print was so faint and muddy that David Twain had to squint hard and hold the sheet of paper up to the light just to make out a few words.

He lowered the folded page and looked around him. People were streaming past on all sides. The students at this school were visibly different. They moved faster. Talked faster. Dressed like they expected a society photographer to show up at any minute. They were, David thought, probably all brain-dead.

Still, nobody else seemed to be having a hard time finding the right room. Of course, the rest of them had spent more than eight minutes in the building.

A bell rang right over his head. The sound of it was so loud that it seemed to jar the fillings in his teeth. David winced and looked up at the clanging bell. That was when he noticed that the number above the door and the room number on the schedule were the same.

A half-dozen students slipped past David as he stood in the doorway. He turned to follow, caught a bare glimpse of movement from the corner of his eye, and the next thing he knew, he was flying through the air.

He landed hard on his butt. All at once he bit his tongue, dropped his brand-new books, and let out a sound that reminded him of a small dog that had been kicked. The books skidded twenty feet, letting out a spray of loose papers as they went.

The bell stopped ringing. In the space of seconds the remaining students in the hallway dived into classrooms. David found himself alone.

`Almost.`

"Sorry."

It was a mumbled apology. Not much conviction there.

David looked up to see a tall girl with loose, tangled blond hair standing over him.

"Yeah," he said. There was a warm, salty taste in his mouth. Blood. And his butt ached from the fall. At the moment those things `didn't matter.`

"You okay?" the girl asked, shoving her hand in her pocket and looking like she'd rather be anywhere but there.

"Yeah," he said again, reaching back to touch his spine. "I'm fine. Great."

The girl shook her head. "If you say so." She offered her hand, even as her face took on an even more sour expression.

Her tousled hair spilled down across her shoulders as she reached to him.

"Thanks." David took her hand and let her help

him to his feet. The girl's palm was warm. Her fingers were surprisingly strong. "What did I run into?"

"Me."

David blinked. "You knocked me down?"

The blond girl shrugged and released his hand. "I didn't do it on purpose."

"You must have been moving pretty fast to hit that hard." David resisted an urge to rub his aches. Instead he offered the hand the girl had just released. "Hi, I'm David Twain."

The girl glanced over her shoulder at the classroom, then stared at David's fingers as if she'd never experienced a handshake before.

"Gaia," she said. "Gaia Moore." She took his hand in hers and gave it a single quick shake.

David was the one who had fallen, but for some reason the simple introduction was enough to make this girl, this painfully beautiful girl, seem awkward.

"Great name," he said. "Like the Earth goddess."

"Yeah, well, if you're okay—"

David shook his head. "No," he said.

Gaia blinked. "What?"

"No," David repeated. "I'm not okay." He leaned toward her and lowered his voice to his best thick whisper. "I won't be okay until you agree to go to dinner with me tomorrow night."

"UH . . . HUH."

The Response

"What?" David asked, his very clear blue eyes narrowing.

He was a male. He was, apparently, a nonfreak. He was not Sam. He got the affirmative grunt before Gaia could remind herself of the ramifications.

"I said, uh-huh," Gaia said evenly, lifting her chin.

"Good," he said. "There's this place called Cookies & Couscous. It's more like a bakery than a restaurant. You know it?"

Of course she knew it. Any place that had *cookies* in its name and was located within twenty miles of her room automatically went on Gaia's mental map.

"On Thompson," she said.

"Right." He nodded, and a piece of black hair fell over his forehead. "We can eat some baklava, wash it down with espresso, and worry about having a main course after we're full of dessert."

For a moment Gaia just looked at him. He was tall. Gangly. Almost sweet looking. Very not Sam.

"Baklava," David repeated with a smirk. "Buttery. Flaky. Honey and nuts."

Gaia nearly smiled. Almost.

This could take her mind off Sam. The kidnappers. The uncle. Heather.

30

"When?" she said.

He smiled. "Tomorrow? Eight o'clock."

Gaia nodded almost imperceptibly.

His smile widened. "It's a date."

And with those words, Gaia's seventeen-year streak officially came to an end.

HEATHER GANNIS COULDN'T BELIEVE

The Unsaid

what she was about to do, but there was no getting around it. There were too many things that had to be said. Things that couldn't go unsaid much longer. Not without Heather going into a paranoid frenzy. And frenzy was not something Heather did well. She liked to be in control. Always.

She looked at her reflection in the scratched bathroom mirror, tossed her glossy brown hair behind her shoulders, took a deep breath, and plunged into the melee that was the post-lunch hall crowd.

Even in the crush of people it only took Heather about five seconds to spot Gaia Moore. And her perfectly tousled blond hair. And her supermodel-tall body. Before she could remind herself of how stupid it was to do this in public, Heather

31

walked right up to Gaia and grabbed her arm.

Gaia looked completely surprised.

"We have to talk," Heather said.

Even more surprised. Gaia yanked her arm away. "Doubtful," she said.

Heather fixed her with a leveling glare as she noticed a few curious bystanders pausing to check out the latest Gaia-Heather confrontation. "Bio lab," Heather said. Then she turned on her heel and made her way to the designated room.

She almost couldn't believe it when Gaia walked in moments later.

Gaia raised her eyebrows and shrugged, tucking her hands into the front pockets of her pants. "Call me curious," she said.

Wanting to remain in charge, Heather slapped her books down on top of one of the big, black tables and rested one hand on her hip. "Who kidnapped Sam?" she asked evenly.

"I don't know," Gaia said, suddenly standing up straight.

"Right," Heather said, her ire already rising. "Then why did they contact you?"

"I don't know," Gaia repeated.

Heather scoffed and looked up at the ceiling, concentrating on trying to keep the blood from rising to her face. "Is that all you're going to say?" she spat. "You asked for my help, then you tripped me on the stairs, and I spent two hours stuck with the idiot police at NYU trying to convince them I wasn't some crazed stalker, and all you can say is, 'I don't know?'" She was sounding hysterical. She had to stop.

Gaia shrugged. It was all Heather could do to keep from clocking the girl in the head with her physics book. She took a long, deep breath through her nose, and let it out slowly—audibly. Then she picked up her books, hugging them to her chest, and walked right up to Gaia, the toe of her suede boot just touching the battered rubber of Gaia's sneaker. The girl didn't move.

"Stay away from Sam," Heather said, trying to muster a threatening tone. It wasn't the easiest thing in the world. Gaia had threatened her. Gaia had hurt her. Gaia had almost gotten her killed.

The girl was like a statue.

Heather stepped around Gaia and headed for the door. She stopped to look behind her and Gaia was frozen in place, as if someone were still standing before her speaking.

"Freak," Heather muttered. And with that, she was out the door.

Before Gaia could snap out of it and come after her.

THE PENCIL SNAPPED. IN THE

silent lecture hall the noise seemed as loud as a gunshot.

Tug-of-War

Thirty pairs of eyes turned toward Sam Moon, and from the back of the hall came a muffled snicker. Sam closed his eyes for a moment, then slowly raised his hand.

"Yes, Mr. Moon," the physics professor said with a tone of tired amusement. "You can get another."

Sam closed his blue test folder and searched quickly through his book bag for a replacement pencil. All around him he could hear the quiet scratching of lead on paper as the rest of the class hurried to complete the exam. Sam's progress on the test couldn't exactly be called hurrying. There were one hundred and twenty questions on the test and exactly fifty-seven minutes to answer them all. With forty-five of those minutes gone, Sam was on number twelve.

He finally located another pencil and put the bag back on the floor. He looked down at the next question, touched the pencil to the paper. The pencil snapped into four pieces.

This time there was nothing muffled about the laughter.

The physics professor, an older man with a comb-over so complex, it was a science in itself, let loose a heavy sigh.

"Mr. Moon, if this test is causing you so much stress, might I suggest you try a pen?" he said with a sneer. "I would not want to be responsible for chopping down whole forests of precious trees just to keep you supplied with pencils."

Sam would have liked to smack the guy. He would have liked to ask him if he'd ever taken a physics midterm two days after being released by a group of as yet unidentified kidnapping psychos. He would have liked to get up and leave the room.

He didn't. Sam Moon did not shirk responsibility. It wasn't in his blood.

Ignoring the remnants of the last wave of laughter, Sam dug through his book bag a second time, extracted a ballpoint, and went back to work. Even the pen gave out a little squeak in his hand, as if the plastic was that close to breaking.

It wasn't just his recent trauma that was causing his tension, although it had less than nothing to do with the exam—less than nothing to do with frequencies and waveforms and photon behavior.

The real tension came from the tug-of-war that was going on in his brain. On one end of the rope was Heather Gannis. The lovely, the popular, the much-sought-after Heather. The Heather that Sam was dating. Assisting on her end of the rope was a whole army of good reasons for Sam to stay in his current relationship. There was beauty—which Heather certainly

35

had. And there was sex, which Heather was willing to provide. And there was a certain reliability. Sam knew Heather. He could count on Heather. He might not always like everything about Heather, but he knew her. There were no surprises on that side.

And of course, she had saved his life.

Dragging the rope in the other direction was Gaia Moore. There was no army on Gaia's side. The girl brought nothing but frustration, confusion, mystery, and imminent danger. Technically she was a mess. And from the moment Sam met her, Gaia had seemed to stumble from one disaster to the next. But at least Gaia wasn't boring. She was anything but.

If Sam's head had staged a fair fight, Team Heather would have dragged Gaia right off the field so fast, she would have had grass burns on her face. But something inside Sam wouldn't let that happen. Something in him kept holding on to Gaia's end of the rope, keeping her in the game.

He closed his eyes for a moment and put his hands against his temples. He had to stop thinking about Gaia. Thinking about Gaia when he was already committed to Heather was wrong. More than that, the way he thought about Gaia all the time was getting to be more than a little like an obsession.

"Ten minutes, people," said the professor. "You should be getting near the end."

Sam shook his head, flinging away the rope and all

its hangers-on. He studied the next question on the test and scribbled out an answer. Then he tackled the next. And the next. When he managed to concentrate, Sam found that the answers came easily. Sometimes it was nice to have the powers of a good geek brain. He sped through a series of equations without faltering, flew past some short answers, and was within five questions of the end when the professor called, "Time."

Sam gathered up his things and carried his paper to the front of the room, relieved. At least he had cleared the Gaia fog from his brain long enough to get some work done. He hadn't embarrassed himself. Not this time, anyway.

But he wasn't sure how long that would last. The battle in his head was still picking up steam. Soon it was going to be a full-blown war.

GAIA STARED DOWN AT THE TOES OF

Maybe Connecticut

her battered sneakers and wondered how long it would be before she threw up. Or ran out of the room. Or exploded.

Accepting a date with a guy she had known all of ten seconds seemed like such a desperate thing. A total loser move. Like something a girl who was seventeen and had never been kissed might do.

The whole thing was starting to make her nauseated.

At least it had already served its purpose. She wasn't thinking about . . . all those things she didn't want to think about.

Who knew what this David guy expected out of her? Gaia the undated. Gaia the untouched. Gaia the ultimate virgin.

Maybe knocking David down had spun his brain around backward. Left him with a concussion that led to his asking out the first girl he saw.

Or maybe it was a setup. Maybe Heather and some of the certified Popular Crowd (also known as The Association of People Who Really Hate Gaia Moore) had put this guy in her way just so they could pop up at her so-called date and pull a *Carrie*.

Gaia closed her eyes and moaned. "Stupid. Definitely stupid."

"Uh, you're Gaia Moore, right?"

Gaia looked up from her desk and found a tall blond girl standing in front of her. From the way people were up and moving around the room, class had to be over. Gaia had successfully managed to obsess away the entire period.

"Are you Gaia?"

"Uh, yeah." Gaia was surprised on two counts. The first was that the girl knew her name at all; the second was that she actually pronounced it right on the first try. "Yeah, that's right."

"I'm Cassie," said the girl. "Cassie Greenman."

How wonderful for you, thought Gaia. She had noticed the girl in class before. Although she hadn't seen her running with the core popular-people crowd, Gaia assumed that Cassie was in on the anti-Gaia coalition.

"Aren't you worried?" Cassie asked.

"What am I supposed to be worried about?" Gaia wondered if she had missed the announcement of a history exam or some similar nonevent. Or maybe this girl was talking about Gaia's upcoming date. Maybe Heather and pals really were planning some horrible heap of humiliation. Maybe they were all standing outside the door right now, ready to mock Gaia for thinking someone would actually ask her out.

Not that Gaia cared.

The girl rolled her eyes. "About being next."

"The next what?" Gaia asked.

"You know." Cassie raised a hand to her throat and drew one silver-blue-painted fingernail across the pale skin of her throat. "Being the next one killed."

Killed. That was a word that definitely drew Gaia's attention. She sat up straighter at her desk. "What do you mean, killed?"

"Killed. Like in dead."

"Killed by who?"

The blond girl shook her head. "By the Gentleman."

Gaia began to wonder if everyone had just gone nuts while she wasn't paying attention. "Why would a gentleman want to kill me?"

"Not *a* gentleman," said Cassie, "*the* Gentleman. You know—the serial killer." She didn't add "duh," but it was clear enough in her voice.

Now Gaia was definitely interested. "Tell me about it."

"Haven't you heard?" Cassie pulled her books a little closer to her chest. "Everyone's been talking about it all morning."

"They haven't been talking to me."

Cassie shrugged. "There's this guy killing girls. He killed two over in New Jersey and three more somewhere in . . . I don't know, maybe Connecticut."

"So?" said Gaia. "Why should I be worried about what happens in Connecticut?"

That drew another roll of the eyes from the blond girl. "Don't you ever listen to the news? Last night he killed a girl from NYU right over on the MacDougal side of the park."

Now Gaia wasn't just interested, she was offended. The park in question was Washington Square Park, and that was Gaia's territory. Her home court.

From the chessboards to the playground, all of

it was hers. She used it as a place to relax and as a place to hunt city vermin. Gaia had been in the park herself the night before, just hoping for muggers and dealers to give her trouble. The idea that someone had been killed just a block away. . . .

"How do they know it was the same guy?" she asked.

"Because of what he . . . does to them," her informant replied with an overdone shiver. "I don't know about you, but I'm dying my hair jet black till this guy is caught."

"Why?"

Cassie was starting to look a little exasperated. She pulled out a lock of her wavy hair and held it in front of her face. "Hello? Because all the victims had the same color hair, that's why. You need to be careful, too."

"I'm not that blond," said Gaia.

"Are you nuts? Your hair's even lighter than mine." The girl gave a little smile. "It's not too different, though. In fact, ever since you started here, people have been telling me how much we look alike. Like you could be my sister or something."

Gaia stared at the girl. Whoever had said she looked like Gaia needed to get their eyes checked. Cassie Greenman was patently pretty. Very pretty. There was no way Gaia looked anything like her.

"You're nothing like me."

Cassie frowned. "You don't think . . ."

"No."

"I think we would look a lot alike," insisted Cassie, "if you would . . . you know . . . like, clean up . . . and dress better. . . ." She shrugged. "You know."

All Gaia knew was that all the cleaning up and good clothes in the world wouldn't stop her from looking like an overmuscled freak. She wished she was beautiful like her mother had been, but she would settle for being pretty like Cassie. She would settle for being normal. "Thanks for giving me the heads up on this killer."

Cassie wrinkled her nose. "Isn't it creepy? Do you think he's still around here?"

"I wouldn't worry too much." Gaia stood up and grabbed for her books. "If he's still here, he won't be for long."

Not in my park, she thought. If the killer was still there, Gaia intended to find him and stop him.

Suddenly she felt pinpricks of excitement moving over her skin. For the first time all day she felt fully awake. Fully engaged. Fully there. She needed to make a plan. She needed to make sure that if this guy attacked anyone else in the park, it was Gaia.

As terrible as it was, in a weird sort of way the news about the serial killer actually made Gaia feel better. At least she had stopped thinking about her date.

"A SERIAL KILLER," ED SAID SLOWLY.

Dead Already

Words he never expected to say unless he was talking about some movie staring Morgan Freeman or Tommy Lee Jones.

Gaia nodded. "That's right."

"And you're excited about this?"

Why was he not surprised?

"Not excited. It's more . . ." She tipped back her head and looked up at the bright blue sky, her breath visible for one split second each time she exhaled. "Yeah, well. Kind of."

Ed stopped talking as they moved around a line of people waiting for a hot dog vendor, then took up the conversation again once he was sure no one was close enough to hear. "Don't you think that's a little—"

"Crazy?" finished Gaia.

"That wasn't what I was going to say." Ed stopped in his tracks and looked up into her eyes, rubbing his gloved hands together. Early November in New York City. Almost time to put away the cotton gloves and whip out the leather. "But since you said it—yeah, it seems more than a little Looney Tunes."

Gaia was silent for a moment. She walked a few steps away and stood next to the fence that bordered the playground. Ed followed.

As usual, the equipment was overrun with bundled-up kids. Anytime between dawn and sunset the playground was packed with screaming children. A little thing like someone getting killed in the park wasn't enough to empty any New York jungle gym. They were too few and far between. The sound of laughter and shouting mixed together with traffic around the park until it was only another kind of white noise – the city version of waves and seagulls at the beach.

"This is important," Gaia said at last. "I have to get this guy."

Ed stared at her, trying to read the expression on her beautiful face. Usually that was easy enough. On an average day Gaia's emotions ran from mildly disturbed to insanely angry. But this expression was something new. Something Ed didn't know how to read. "Does this have something to do with Sam's kidnapping?" he asked. "Why exactly do you have to . . . get him?"

Why and you being the operative words.

Gaia pushed at her tangled hair to get it out of her face but only succeeded in tangling it further. "Because I do," she said, looking down at him. "And I don't think this has anything to do with Sam. This guy is killing blond girls, not college guys. But this also isn't just some loser snatching purses or some asshole junkie waving a knife to feed a crack habit. This is serious."

"Some of those assholes kill people," Ed pointed

out, tucking his hands under his arms. "Stopping them is important, too."

"Yeah, but not like this. This guy, this *Gentleman*, he's killing people because he wants to do it." She stared out at the kids on the swing sets, and Ed saw that her ever-changing eyes had turned a shade of blue that was almost electric. "This guy likes what he's doing."

Ed was chilled to the bone. He blamed it on the sudden, stiff breeze that picked up dead leaves and general city debris all around them. But he knew it was more about Gaia's words.

"What do you know about this guy?" he asked.

Gaia shrugged, hooking her bare fingers around the metal links of the fence. "Nothing, really. He kills blond girls. I'm not sure how many."

"Why is he called the Gentleman?" Ed asked.

"I don't know that, either. I don't really know anything about him . . . yet."

There was one particularly loud playground scream, and Gaia's eyes darted left, searching for possible trouble.

Ed ignored the kids and stared at Gaia's profile. Looking at her was something he always enjoyed, but this time he was looking with a purpose. He hadn't known Gaia for that long, but he had never seen her back away from anything she set out to do. From what he could read of the expression on her face, Gaia was

45

determined to stop this killer. Ed could either get behind her or get out of the way.

"Maybe I could help you," he said.

Gaia shook her head. She didn't even look at him. "I don't want you getting hurt."

Ed tried hard not to be insulted. "Hey, we've been through this before. I'm not going to be out here playing Jackie Chan. That's your job. I just thought I could help you fill in the holes."

"Holes?"

"Holes." He tilted his head in an attempt to catch her eyes. "Like I did with Sam."

She blinked, and her grip on the fence tightened. There. She couldn't deny he'd been indispensable when Sam was kidnapped. He'd figured out where they were holding Sam—not that the information had played a role in rescuing him. But he'd helped Gaia get the key to Sam's room from Heather—not that they'd needed it. But he *had* caused a distraction so that Gaia could sneak into the dorm. Of course, if he hadn't been there, she probably wouldn't have needed a distraction in the first place, but—

"Ed—"

"Let me at least read up on the guy," Ed interrupted before she could shoot him down. "Maybe I can figure out what he's about. What he's got against girls with pigment-challenged hair."

Gaia turned away from the kids and knelt down

next to the chair. It was a move that usually made Ed angry—he didn't want people bending down beside him like he was a three-year-old—but anything that brought Gaia Moore's face closer to his own was an okay move in Ed's book.

"Okay," she said. "But you do research. *Only* research. I do the . . . other. Maybe together we can exterminate this guy."

We. Together. Ed liked the sound of that. It wasn't just Gaia going after a killer. It was Gaia and Ed. Batman and Robin. Partners.

"All right," he agreed. "I'll dig into the Net. Maybe stop by the library."

"Good," Gaia said. She smiled. In a strained way.

Forced or not, two smiles in one day from Gaia Moore had to be a record. Still, something about this whole thing had Ed moderately wiggy.

"Want me to call you tonight?" he asked.

"I'll call you," Gaia said. She started walking again, and Ed hurried to keep up. "If you can get some info in the next couple of hours, maybe I can bag this loser before he moves on to a different neighborhood."

She made a sound that might almost have been a laugh and ran the long fingers of her right hand through the heavy mass of her tangled hair. "Besides, I'm busy tomorrow night."

"What's tomorrow?" Ed asked.

"I've got a date." Gaia glanced over at Ed. For a split second she looked small, vulnerable. Like what he was about to say mattered. Unfortunately, Ed's heart was in his mouth, temporarily making speech impossible.

"A date," Ed replied finally. "Wow." Articulate, it was not, but he was pleased to hear that his voice sounded normal. He even managed to keep a smile on his face.

But if the serial killer came for him, Ed wouldn't have to be afraid. He felt dead already.

Girls I have liked:
Jenn Challener
Aimee Eastwood
Raina Korman
Ms. Reidy
Jennifer Love Hewitt (Okay, I
was fourteen)
Storm, Rogue, Jubilee, Jean Grey
The lady behind the counter at
Balducci's

Girls I have loved:
Heather Gannis
Gaia Moore

**Girls who have ripped out my
  cardiovascular muscle and
squashed it under their feet:**
Heather Gannis
Gaia Moore

Anyone besides me sensing a
pattern around here?

One glance from afar was all he needed. But he needed it like he needed oxygen.

the gaia flu

THE PARK WAS JUST A SHORTCUT.

Give in to Insanity

The fastest way from point A to point B.

Besides, cutting through the park would take Sam past the chess tables. Not that he had time for a game, but it never hurt to see who was playing. He had to keep up on the competition. See who was new. Check out who was winning, who was losing. It wasn't like he was looking for anyone in particular. Nope. Not at all.

Except that he was.

Truth? Sam was sneaking through the park, looking for Gaia. Not to meet her, not to talk to her, just to *see* her. One glance from afar was all he needed. But he needed it like he needed oxygen.

Before Sam met Gaia, the park had seemed like the one safe place in his life. Sure, it was a hangout for muggers and junkies, scam artists, aging hippies, and gang members. If you wandered off the path on the wrong day or stayed too long on the wrong night, you could be beat up, maimed, or even killed. Every place had dangerous people, but Washington Square Park had more than its share.

Sam knew about that firsthand.

But none of that stopped him from loving the place. When he was hanging out in the park, he could relax. Nobody at the chess tables cared if he wore the right things, said the right things, or hung with the right people. Playing chess in the park was one situation where Sam could lean back and let his inner geek rise to the surface.

Gaia had ruined that.

From the first time they played, Sam had developed this weird kind of spastic tick. No matter who he was playing, every ten seconds Sam had to look up from the board to see if he might catch a glimpse of blond hair flying loose in the wind or a beautiful face centered around a scowl.

Sam had seen plenty of stories about obsessive-compulsive people. People who can't leave the house without locking the door ten times or who wash their hands a hundred times a day. He just hadn't expected to become one of those people. Glance at the chessboard, look around for Gaia. Move a piece. Check for Gaia. It was more than sick. It was pathetic.

What was worse was that he had no idea how he really felt about Gaia. Sam had good reasons to hate her—had once even told her he hated her—and the kidnapping should have only made him hate her more.

The kidnapping. Something Sam was trying so hard not to think about even though the questions kept flashing through his mind at warp speed.

Why me?

What did they want?

Did they get it?

Who were they?

Why did they let me go?

And, of course, what did Gaia have to do with the whole thing?

He'd been chasing Gaia when it happened. And he had the vague, possibly imagined memory of Gaia's named being mentioned by one of the kidnappers while he was semiconscious and half dead on a concrete floor. That was the thought that always gave him pause.

Kidnappers mentioning Gaia = kidnappers knowing Gaia = Gaia having something to do with the torture he was put through = Sam should hate Gaia.

But Sam was pretty sure that wasn't how he felt. If it was hate, it was a weird kind. Still, this obsession couldn't be love. It was more like an illness. The Gaia flu. Gaia-itis.

If she had anything to do with what happened to him, she must have been just as much a victim as he was. That had to be it.

Suddenly Sam found himself carefully scanning the park.

He was looking for her now—going out of his way and looking. This wasn't just the possibility of a random encounter anymore. And he was supposed to be on his way to meet his girlfriend.

Sam tucked his chin and kept walking. Eyes down. Hands in pockets. Too bad he didn't have side blinders like the horses that drew carriages through Central Park.

He needed a cure for this disease. Brain surgery. `Strong anti-Gaiotics.` At the very least, a good psychiatrist.

When he got to the chess tables, Sam found them almost deserted. Only a handful of regulars were playing, taking money from the usual mix of naive college students and overconfident businessmen who strolled through the park. A couple of would-be players were sitting across from empty seats, hoping for fresh victims.

No Gaia.

Sam felt `a swirling mixture of disappointment and relief.` It was kind of like the feeling he got when someone else took the last scoop of Ben & Jerry's. It was probably good for him to skip that ten zillion additional calories; it just didn't feel good at all.

Zolov was at his table, of course. He was in the middle of a game, so Sam didn't stop to talk. Not that talking would have bothered Zolov. Zolov might be a little crazy, but he knew how to concentrate on chess.

A middle-aged Pakistani looked at Sam with a hopeful expression. "You want a game, Sam?"

He shook his head. "Not today, Mr. Haq. Sorry."

"Oh, sit down and play," the part-time taxi driver, full-time chess hustler said. "It won't take long."

When Sam considered the way he'd been playing lately, that part was probably true. "Sorry, I really don't have time."

Since Sam had become Gaia infected, he had become Mr. Popularity at the chess tables. Everyone wanted to play him. He had lost money to people he used to put down in ten minutes.

Past the chess tables, Sam picked up the pace. Heather wasn't the kind of girl who took well to waiting.

Sam slipped through the not-so-miniature marble Arc de Triomphe at the center of the park and was almost out of the park. Then he saw her.

Gaia was thirty feet away, talking to a guy in a wheelchair. He recognized the guy. It was Ed Fargo, Heather's ex. But Sam didn't spend any time looking at Ed. That would be a waste of Gaia time.

Her hair was light and golden in the sunlight. Sam couldn't tell what Gaia was saying, but her face was incredibly animated. Even from where he was standing, Sam imagined he could see the deep, shifting blue of Gaia's eyes. A little gray in the center. Streaks that were almost turquoise. It was only imagination, but he had a very good imagination when it came to Gaia.

For just a moment another image of Gaia started to seep into Sam's mind. An image of Gaia in the dark, leaning over him, urgently whispering to him. Sam's heart froze in his chest.

The kidnapping.

He knew that couldn't be right. It was Heather who had come in at the last second to save Sam and give him the insulin he so desperately needed. Not Gaia. Still, there was something about the events that scratched at the insides of his skull.

The path Gaia was walking angled away from Sam. If he stood there for another ten seconds, she would be out of sight. To keep up with her, all he had to do was take ten fast steps. Another ten steps and he would catch her.

All he had to do was forget Heather, forget everything, and follow Gaia. All he had to do was give in to insanity.

Sam took the first step.

HEATHER LOOKED AGAIN AT THE watch on her wrist. Time. Time and then some.

Times Ten

She stretched her neck, looking around for Sam. Heather wished he hadn't asked her to meet him at the entrance of the park. She didn't have to go inside, but even the sidewalk was still way too close.

Heather didn't like the park. She had been cut

there, almost killed by some maniac. Since then she had looked at the clumps of trees and clutter of equipment as hiding places for thieves, murderers, and worse. It didn't surprise Heather that some brainless girl had gotten herself killed there. She was only surprised that it didn't happen more often.

The park held monsters. She was sure of it.

Heather checked her watch again. Ten minutes late. If it had been anyone but Sam, she would have left. She was beginning to wonder if she had the place or time wrong when Sam suddenly stepped into view. Heather put on her best smile and raised her hand in a little wave.

Sam didn't respond. He was walking right toward Heather, but he didn't even seem to see her. There was a distant, distracted look on his face. His curly, ginger-colored hair seemed a little more mussed than usual. Even his normally crisp tweed jacket looked wrinkled. Heather didn't appreciate the change.

Sam had been ill, and of course, there was the whole kidnapping thing, but still. He needed to take better care of himself. After all, appearance was very important. Sam knew that.

Sam took two more steps, stopped, and looked into the park.

For a moment Heather worried that Sam might really be sick again. Or maybe he had been attacked. There was a confused, stunned expression on his face.

Maybe some lunatic in the park had hit him on the head. Maybe he was hurt.

Heather started walking toward him quickly. She was almost close enough to touch him when Sam moved again. But he didn't come toward Heather. He stepped off the path and into the grass.

Heather frowned. "Sam?"

Sam jumped. He whipped around and stared at Heather with wide eyes.

"Um. Uh." He stopped and cleared his throat. "Heather."

The way he said it made it seem like he was surprised to see her. Heather couldn't put her finger on it, but something about his expression irritated her. A slight blush tinted her cheeks. She crossed her arms over her chest.

"What's wrong, Sam? Are you okay?" She tried to sound concerned and earnest. It came out as defensive and accusatory. Luckily, Mr. Oblivious didn't seem to notice.

Sam nodded quickly. "Yeah, sure. I just . . ." His face suddenly flushed an incredible bright red. "I just got lost in thought."

Heather's eyebrows scrunched together. She tried to smile again, but it was more difficult this time. "Oookay," she said. "C'mon. Let's get out of here."

Lacing her fingers with Sam's, Heather started to lead him out of the park. He was coming out of the bizarre stupor—walking like a normal person instead of shuffling like he had moments before. In fact, within seconds he was practically pulling her arm out of its socket.

What was with him? He was acting like something had him spooked. Heather glanced back in the direction Sam had been looking when he'd stopped in place. For a fraction of a second, a moment so short it might have been imagination, Heather thought she saw someone stepping behind a group of trees—someone with pale blond hair.

Heather's blood went cold and hot at the same time. It had only been the barest glimpse, but she knew who that blond hair belonged to. Gaia Moore. And Sam didn't want Heather to see her.

"Sam? What's the rush?" Heather said, just to see if ne would tell her the truth.

"Nothing," he said, still pulling.

Heather felt a familiar feeling of humiliation, mixed with anger and tinged with fear, slip through her veins. God, she hated Gaia. Heather hated Gaia more than she had ever hated anyone in her whole life. More than everyone she had ever hated in her life put together. Times ten.

Sam stopped pulling when they reached the far corner, but Heather kept her hand locked together with his as they strolled down the sidewalk. Sam was saying something to her, making suggestions about where they might go, what they might do. Heather gave vague, one-word answers to his questions without really hearing them. It was her turn to be distracted.

Since her first encounter with Gaia, Heather had been burned, humiliated, stabbed, hospitalized, ego bruised, deprived of her boyfriend on various occasions, and detained by the NYU security force.

None of that came close to the reason Heather hated Gaia. It was the way Sam acted around Gaia. Like he couldn't think or breathe. Like he'd never seen anything like her.

And then there was the fact that Gaia was beautiful. She was beautiful without even trying. And that brought Heather to the real heart of it. Not the beauty. Heather hated Gaia because she didn't seem to try, didn't seem to care what others thought of her. Gaia dressed like a refugee. She said whatever she wanted. She never even seemed to notice how guys turned around to watch her when she went by. Gaia acted like she didn't think she was pretty, but Heather knew better than that. Gaia had to know. She just didn't care.

It was driving Heather mad—in every sense of the word.

Sam suddenly stopped walking. His grip on Heather's hand tightened to painful intensity.

Heather came out of her daze and struggled against his tight grip. "Sam? Sam, what's wrong?"

"Nothing," he replied in a harsh whisper. He

stopped again and shook his head. "Nothing. Don't worry about it."

Heather stared at him. For a moment she had a terrible premonition that everything between them was over. Ice went down her spine, trickling slowly over every lump in her backbone. *He's going to tell me he's dumping me. Dumping me for Gaia Moore.*

But Sam wasn't even looking at Heather. She followed the direction of his gaze and saw a newspaper stand. Right away Heather spotted the thing that had captured Sam's attention.

Splashed across the front page of the *Post* was a color photo of a young blond girl. Under the picture was the caption KILLER TAKES 6TH VICTIM.

Heather untangled her fingers from Sam's and went in for a closer look. From a distance, the girl in the picture looked a lot like Gaia. A tabloid twin. This had to be the girl that the serial killer had murdered the night before, the one that everyone had been talking about at school.

It wasn't Gaia. Still, Heather felt a little thrill go through her. As sick as she knew the thought was, the idea of Gaia and murder just seemed so right.

NEW YORK POST

ANOTHER BLOND BEAUTY DEAD
Gentleman Killer Plants Bloody Knife in Heart of NYC

After a killing spree that has left victims scattered from Connecticut to New Jersey, the serial killer known only as the "Gentleman" has taken his act off Broadway—slicing up an NYU coed just a block from the school's campus.

Carolyn Mosley, 20, a freshman at NYU, was found dead this morning by maintenance workers at Washington Square Park, say city officials. The manner of death points to a connection with the string of killings committed by the infamous serial killer, the Gentleman, according to officials.

Police have been reluctant to share details of the killer's technique, but sources have confirmed that this Gentleman is no gentleman. Death in the Gentleman's victims has been brought about by numerous knife wounds, according to information released by New Jersey police. Victims have received multiple stab wounds and have suffered "extreme violence and extensive damage," according to reports on the previous victims.

"Their throats were cut so badly, they were nearly decapitated," said Stanley G. Norster, a detective who investigated the Gentleman's killings in Connecticut. "There's an incredible amount of anger in these killings. A rage."

Police have admitted to withholding some details of the Gentleman's actions in previous crimes. The FBI has been involved in this investigation for several weeks, and a psychological profile of the killer has been prepared, but this profile has not been made available to the public. Sources inside the coroner's office indicate that the bodies show evidence of torture. The killer apparently administered dozens of cuts and other injuries before the killing blow. The killer didn't stop with death. Other signs

Continued on page 12

NYU Student Killed in Washington Square Park

NYU—A New York University student was found dead early this morning only two blocks from the university campus, according to police. Carolyn Mosley, 20, a freshman at NYU, died as a direct result of blunt trauma and numerous stab wounds, officials say.

The body was discovered in the southwestern part of Washington Square Park by maintenance workers responding to a report of a gas leak. No leak was found, but Ms. Moser's body was found at the location of the alleged leak. Police spokesmen refused comment when asked about the possibility that the gas leak was reported by someone involved in the murder.

Mosley was last seen leaving a restaurant on MacDougal Street around 11 P.M., according to officials. The student worked part-time at the restaurant and worked her regular shift there the evening of her death.

No suspects have been named; however, the condition of the body has led to speculation that the case may be related to a series of killings in Connecticut.

Police have scheduled a press conference for 3 P.M. to discuss the case. Case files from the possibly related murders in other states have been requested, according to police.

From: E.
To: L.

    Last night's events confirm Delta presence. High probability of encounter with primary subject and subsequent risk. Advise.

From: L.
To: E.

    Continue to monitor activity. Do not intercede at this time. Will personally visit site within twenty-four hours.

    I want to see what happens.

They had nothing
in common at
all—nothing

numbering

except a general **the**
similarity
of features **dead**
and the fact
that they were
all dead.

ONE AFTER ANOTHER, THE FACES

Pretty Girls

and names of the Gentleman's victims appeared on the computer monitor.

Debra Lemasters—more cute than beautiful, with her hair pulled back in a ponytail and wide blue eyes that stared out from a yearbook photo.

Amanda Loring—older, taller. Holding a track trophy aloft while teammates cheered.

Susan Creek—eyes more gray than blue, thinner than the rest. She looked so sad, it was almost as if she knew what was coming.

Clarissa Richardson—very pretty but looking awfully uncomfortable in a tight, off-the-shoulder formal gown and a paper crown that proclaimed her queen of the junior prom.

Paulina Dree—sitting on horseback, her father standing beside her, both smiling. She had a great smile.

And finally, poor Carolyn Mosley, posing in cap and gown, a high school diploma rolled in her hand. Valedictorian of her class. Her family's pride and joy.

The youngest of them was fifteen, the oldest, twenty. They were six young women from three different states. None of them had known one another. Most but not all were good students. Most but not all had participated in some sort of organized athletics. They shared no common hobbies. They didn't read the same books, or like the same music, or share the same dreams.

They had nothing in common at all—nothing except a general similarity of features and the fact that they were all dead. And blond hair.

Gaia's hair, thought Tom Moore. He scrolled through the pictures again.

If he looked closely, he could see a little of Gaia in each of the dead girls. It was far more than the hair. The dead girls weren't identical, but they shared a similar bone structure—wide eyes, strong cheekbones, high forehead. Pretty girls, all of them. Of course, Tom was sure that none of them was as pretty as Gaia. But then again, Tom might be more than a little prejudiced—he thought his daughter was the most beautiful young woman in the world.

Six dead girls who all looked a little like Gaia Moore.

"What have they done?" Tom whispered to the empty room. He leaned back from the monitor and stared into the shadows. "What have *we* done?"

IT NEVER GOT DARK IN THE CITY.

Not really dark the way it had in other places. Like Connecticut.

He strolled down the sidewalk, careful never to touch

Warm-up Exercises

anyone he passed. He didn't like to touch people. He didn't like to be touched.

The sun was already going down, but the sky overhead only shifted from blue to a kind of dingy yellow as the lights came on. It wasn't anything close to real darkness. After only three days in the city, he still thought the dirty, nearly starless sky seemed terribly odd.

He craved the darkness.

He moved off the sidewalk and headed down the curving path that led out under the trees. A handful of children were still indulging in a few last minutes of play, but there were parents on hand to watch and a policeman standing at the edge of the playground. A pair of street musicians were putting away their instruments and counting up handfuls of change and folded bills.

They were scared. All of them were scared of the coming night.

He could feel it, almost taste it. For a moment he had a desire to rush into the center of them, screaming and waving his arms, just so he could watch them scatter. He fought down that desire.

No matter how fun it might be to see them run, it wasn't his reason for being in the park. There was important work to be done—a higher purpose. Nothing could be allowed to get in the way of that purpose.

He walked on, passing two more policemen on his way to the chess tables. Like the playground, the boards were almost deserted. Two men still squinted at a game in the failing light. At another table an old man slowly packed away his chess pieces.

The old man looked up as he passed. "You wanting game?" he said. "I will play you."

"No, thanks, Gramps." The idea of playing this guy actually made him smile. The man was ridiculously ancient, with sun-spotted skin and flyaway tufts of white hair. Beating him at chess couldn't possibly be a challenge.

Killing him would be even easier.

It would be a mercy, really. Put the old fool out of his misery. Maybe he would do it. Not as a main course for the evening, but just as a warm-up exercise. Something to keep his fingers busy.

The old man shuffled away, and the moment passed. Pointless, anyway. It was no fun without a real struggle.

He moved away from the tables and down the tree-lined paths. Even in the middle of the park there was nothing that approached true darkness.

But under the trees and in the shaded places, it was dark enough for his purposes.

The form on
the ground
didn't even
look like a
girl. It **chalk**
barely
looked like
a person.

DEATH DIDN'T LEAVE MUCH OF A

permanent stain. Not on the
park, at least.

Stalking a Stalker

Gaia reached out and caught
a strip of the yellow tape in her
hand. Crime Scene—Do Not
Cross.

As if yellow tape created
some magical force field that could keep everyone
away. Gaia wondered if police tape had ever stopped
anybody in the history of the world from jumping into
the middle of a crime site. The temptation was just too
much. Even when you weren't stalking a stalker.

Considering how everyone had been talking up the
murder at school and in the papers, Gaia had expected
to find the park swarming with cop types. She had
thought there would be uniforms keeping back the
crowds. Whole squadrons of trench-coat-wearing detectives combing the ground, examining every blade
of grass for a clue like a flock of investigat-
ing sheep. There should have been technicians
spreading fingerprint powder. Flashing lights. Enough
doughnuts to soak up a swimming pool of coffee.

Instead there was only this dark patch
of grass. If there had been detectives, they were
long gone. There wasn't a single cop left to keep people from ignoring the warning on the flimsy yellow
tape. No one had even left behind a doughnut.

Losers.

Still, Gaia had a hard time stepping over the line. It wasn't like she was afraid of getting caught. Gaia didn't do afraid.

Maybe it was some new desire to be a law-abiding citizen. She wasn't sure. But the idea of going across the tape, going to the place where the body had been, made Gaia feel weird. Like something way down inside her wasn't quite as solid as it should be. Squishy.

She stood there and took a few deep breaths of evening air before the squishiness started to fade. After all, there was nothing out there but grass.

Gaia ducked under the tape. Inside the magic line the ground was all dented and bumpy—like it had been walked on by a herd of elephants. Maybe there really had been hundreds of detecto-sheep here after all.

The grass in the field was soaked with dew. By the time she'd taken a dozen steps, Gaia's sneakers were soaked through and cold water was making little burping noises between her toes. A lovely way to start a long evening.

Almost dead center in the field she saw the rough outline of a body marked in white. Just like in the movies. Only this line wasn't made from tape. It was powdered, chalky stuff, like they use to mark the baselines at a ball game.

Somewhere in the back of Gaia's head, random associations started to fire.

Strike three. You're out. Game over.

When she considered where she was standing, this seemed more than a little sick. But Gaia had never claimed to be in complete control of what went on in her head.

She stood with the toes of her wet sneaks almost touching the crumbling chalk line. The form on the ground didn't even look like a girl. It barely looked like a person. It was just a rough outline with something like a hand pointing one way and two blocky leg things shooting off the other end.

Despite all the violence Gaia had seen in her life— despite all the violence she had caused—there was something about this scene that gave her pause. She wasn't scared; she just felt ill. Ill and numb and . . . responsible. And sad. Where there had been a girl with warmth and memories and a smile, there was now just chalk and dew. It was almost too much for her.

Gaia turned away, wanting to block out the images of premature dying, but her eyes were drawn back as if some unseen thing were pulling her.

Gaia was no big believer. She didn't go in for ghosts, or voodoo, or little leprechauns with colored marshmallow cereal. If people wanted to call themselves witches, that was cool with Gaia as long as they didn't expect her to believe in witchcraft. She might be an overmuscled, fear-deprived, jump-kicking freak girl, but Gaia didn't skim the tabloids for predictions or use a Ouija board to communicate with the dead. For all the weirdness in her life, she knew where to draw the line between what was real and what was not. Or at least, she thought she did.

But the area inside the police tape gave Gaia a bad feeling. Something worse than a mugging or robbery had happened there. And Gaia could still feel it.

She looked up from the line on the ground and did a quick check of the trees around her—just in case any werewolves or zombies were approaching. Then she laughed at herself.

Still, he could be out there. Right there.

There was that whole bad film noir/cheesy paper-back theory that criminals return to the scene of the crime.

It sounded like an idea dreamed up by a lazy detective or by some writer who didn't know where to go with the plot. Just sit on your ass, and the killer will come to you. In Gaia's book that was way too easy to be true.

There was no real reason to think the killer might come back to this place. None at all. Gaia had the whole park to patrol. She couldn't stand here all night, staring at an empty field. Glaring at the trees made about as much sense as her Sam obsession.

But when she looked again, something was out there. Right at the bottom of a bunch of little ash trees, stuck in a chunk of shadow was—something. Maybe someone.

The all-over sickness she had been feeling started to turn into the more familiar `let's-go-kick-some-ass buzz.` Gaia took a slow step toward the shape in the shadows. She squinted until her eyes watered. Was someone really there? She couldn't be sure. She took another step. It was so hard to see. The shape in the shadows could be a crouching person, or it could be a shrub or a trash can.

Then the shape moved.

HE WAS UP AND RUNNING BEFORE

she had a chance to blink. There was no reason to run, really. He could just kill her now.

`He wasn't afraid of her.`

No Killing Tonight

But he was in the mood for a challenge. He wanted to run. Run until it hurt. Until the air coming in and out of his lungs burned the delicate flesh of his throat.

He wanted her to feel the same thing.

And so he ran. There was no way she would catch up to him. Which meant no killing tonight. But that was okay.

He wanted to see what she could do.

Gaia vs. Bad Guy

GAIA'S LEGS WERE PUMPING EVEN before her brain had finished realizing that it really was a person out there. Someone had been there in the shadows, watching her. Now the person was running. So was Gaia.

She made it out of the chewed-up field and jumped the police tape on the far side. For a moment she stood there, frustration tightening her throat. It was a terrible thing to be ready for a fight and not find anyone to punch.

Then she saw the shadow guy again. He was a hundred feet away, cutting across the grass by the side of the path. Gaia started after him.

Then something strange happened.

The average Gaia-versus-bad-guy race lasted all of five seconds. It wasn't that she was Ms. Olympic Runner, but the same thing that made Gaia strong also made her pretty damn fast in a sprint. Her father said it was part of being fearless. That little regulator that keeps people from pushing their muscles to the absolute limit was absent without leave in Gaia. She could push her legs a hundred percent. Maybe further. Gaia could even push her muscles so hard that she broke her own bones.

Disgusting but true.

There was a price to pay for beating herself up like that, but the upside was irresistible—before Gaia began to fade, most losers were on the pavement.

Not this guy. Shadow Man was fast. More than fast. A real speed demon.

Gaia and the shadow whipped along the path through the heart of the park, jumped a hedge, and skirted a gnarled old oak. Gaia didn't gain a step. She could never get close enough to see more than a hazy form in the distance. Several times she almost convinced herself that nothing was out there but shadows—no man at all. But she didn't stop.

By now Gaia was solidly in the zone. Nothing mattered in the world but catching the guy in the shadows. The chessboards came and went in a blur. The playground. The sprinklers. Then they were out of the park, powering north on Fifth Avenue.

In the back of her mind nagged the vague thought that she had no clear reason to pursue him except for the fact that he was running away from her. But the chase was on, and her instincts pushed her hard to catch him.

She zipped past knots of people and saw startled faces turning her way. A woman jumped back as Gaia thundered past. A guy dropped a bag of groceries, and apples went bouncing along the sidewalk.

Gaia didn't slow. They had been running now for a solid minute at a speed that would have been impressive for a ten-second sprint. Her chest heaved in and out as she tried to draw in all the air in New York.

Then she realized she was gaining on the shadow. Not much, but the gap was definitely closing.

Another hundred yards and she had gotten close enough to see that he was wearing some kind of long, floppy black coat. Not a trench coat, but something from a cowboy movie. A duster.

How could he run this fast in that thing?

Gaia followed as the duster flapped past the trendy crowd waiting outside Clementine's, past the glowing signs at Starbuck's, and on across fourteenth Street without even looking at the streams of passing traffic. Her heartbeat seemed to move up through her body with every step. One moment it was pounding against Gaia's ribs. The next it was beating in her throat. The next it was throbbing in her skull.

Shadow Man took a hard right onto a side street, then ducked down an alley. Gaia was right behind him. The gap between the two runners had closed to no more than fifty feet. Forty.

A mesh fence blocked one end of the alley. Gaia slowed a step, getting ready to fight, but the guy in the black coat didn't hesitate. He jumped up, landed one foot on a Dumpster, and sprang from there to the top of the fence. Two steps and he was over the ten-foot barrier. He hit the other side running.

"*What?*" Gaia gasped.

She might not get scared, but she was still quite capable of being amazed.

Gaia ran up to the fence, looped her hands in the mesh, and flung herself upward. She flipped head over heels and her feet came down on the top of the gate. A very slick move.

Then the top of the gate sagged, and she fell.

The pavement wasn't friendly to Gaia's knee. She hit with a force that sent jolts of fire running up her thigh and set off flares of white light in her head.

Gaia stayed there for the space of two breaths. Then she got on her feet and ran again.

Black Coat had widened his lead on Gaia to a good hundred feet, but she soon had it back to fifty. He cut right again, this time along University Place. Gaia followed.

The pair sprinted past a series of nightclubs. The door of each one spilled out different music, but Gaia went past them so fast, they blended like notes in some insane song. Disco high C. Jazz G. Bass blues.

Thirty feet.

Shadow Man was wearing running shoes. Gaia could see them now. The off-white soles flashed at her under the flapping hem of his long coat. She found something comforting about the shoes. At least it was nice to know he wasn't running so fast in penny loafers.

Twenty feet.

A policewoman shouted at Gaia as she dashed across Fourteenth Street and headed south. She didn't bother to stop. If the policewoman wanted Gaia, she had better start running.

Now Gaia realized the man had brought her right back to Washington Square Park, and they ran through shadows cast by huge oaks and ghost white birch.

Ten feet.

Gaia could almost reach out and touch the flapping coat. Almost. The air in her throat tasted like fire, and there were little sparks of white light dancing in her eyes. In another ten seconds this psycho was hers.

Then somebody screamed.

Gaia thought for a second it was her. She was hurting badly enough to scream.

Then the sound came again from somewhere off to her right.

Five feet.

All Gaia had to do was keep running and she could catch the black coat. But what if she caught him and he turned out to be innocent? Really fast, but innocent.

What if the Gentleman was killing someone else in the park right that second? Gaia tried to get her oxygen-starved brain to make a decision. Another scream.

"Oh, shit," she wheezed through her breathing.

Gaia turned right, leaving Black Coat to run on into the night, and dashed toward the commotion.

It didn't take her ten seconds to find who was doing the screaming. Standing under a pool of light was a young girl in blue jeans and a black sweater. Tugging on her purse strap was a potbellied, long-haired guy with a tangled brown-and-gray beard that went halfway down his chest. The girl had both hands clamped to her purse and her feet well planted. She was putting everything she had into it. The guy might outweigh her by a good fifty pounds, but she was giving him a fight.

"Let go!" the girl cried.

The guy laughed. "Come on, baby. I need it worse than you."

Gaia didn't think either one of them saw her coming. By then she was running at roughly the speed of a 747 pulling out of JFK. Gaia didn't slow a bit as she tucked in her head, lowered a shoulder, and smashed into Brown Beard.

The impact was enough to make Gaia fall to her bruised knee and send fresh neon bolts of pain ripping through her body. The bearded guy was knocked at least ten feet. He lay facedown on the grass with one hand stretched out over his head and the other trapped under his body. For just a second Gaia flashed back to the chalk outline on the ground. Hand up, legs spread.

She shook her aching head to clear away some of the fog and climbed to her feet. It seemed like a long way up.

"Y-You . . . ," Gaia started, then took a breath and tried again. "You okay?" she asked the girl.

The girl nodded. Gaia couldn't see her clearly, but she was very tall and very slim. Delicate looking. And she was definitely young. Way too young to be walking around the park alone at night. Of course, who was Gaia to talk?

"Who are you?" the girl asked.

"I—" Gaia couldn't think of a good answer. If she even had a name, she had misplaced it somewhere.

Somewhere back along the long minutes and longer miles of her run. Gaia turned around and staggered back the way she had come.

"Where are you going?" the girl called.

Gaia didn't bother to answer. There wasn't enough air to talk and run.

She put up her arms, drew in a deep breath, and started back to the spot where she had last seen the shadow man.

Gaia made maybe three whole steps before the ground jumped up and gave her a hard slap in the face.

You'd think that I wouldn't
have a very vivid imagination.
I'm a science geek, right? I play
chess. It's all analytical. It's
all about numbers, proofs,
strategies.

Solid definitions.

There's no room for imagination.

But sometimes I don't even believe what my mind can come up
with. There are things living in
my head I'm sure any shrink worth
his cheap spiral notepad would
kill to delve into.

My imagination is especially
vivid when it comes to Gaia
Moore.

And not in the way you think.
I'm not a total pervert.
Although . . . Well, yes, the
brain does travel in those circles, but I'm a guy. You have to
forgive it.

I'm talking about the sick
side of my mind. The dark side.
The side a lot of people probably
have but don't talk about. And

ever since this afternoon, that
side has been transmitting Gaia
pictures. Not pleasant Gaia pictures.

Pictures of Gaia dead. Pictures
of Gaia cut. Pictures of Gaia
bleeding and crying and gasping
and sputtering. They only last
for seconds at a time before I
drive them away. But in those
seconds they scare me to death.
They arrest every functioning
part of my body and take the
breath out of me.

Why?

Because they could become reality.

Ed stared at
the handset in
confusion.

"Who is this?"

the
connection

"Sam Moon,"
said the voice.
"I'm trying to
reach Ed."

ED HIT THE KEYS ON HIS COMPUTER

so hard, the whole desk started shaking. The words on the word processor screen glowed back at him.

Serial Killer Junkie

```
LOSER. LOSER.
LOSER. BIG LOSER. ALL THOUGHT AND NO ACTION MAKES
ED ONE GIANT LOSER. LOSER. LOSER.
```

Somewhere, three screens' worth of LOSERs away, there was a letter that started with "Dear Gaia." It was a letter that explained everything. It was a letter that put into words all the things Ed wished he could have said that morning.

LOSER, Ed typed one last time, moving his fingers slowly across the keys and striking each one as if he meant to knock a letter from the keyboard.

```
L. O. S. E. R.
```

He closed his eyes for a moment and rubbed at his temples. It turned out that losing, or at least not getting the woman you loved, caused a massive headache. Three aspirins had gone down his throat and Ed still felt like his skull was going to bust wide open. He almost wished it would.

With a sigh he moved the mouse up to the corner of his document and clicked the close button.

Save changes? the machine asked.

Ed clicked on the No button and watched as both his letter to Gaia and his three-page tribute to self-pity blinked into nothing.

He took in a deep breath, turned his back to the computer, and rolled over to the heap of books lying on his bed.

He had braved the snarling stone lions and endless wheelchair ramps at the main public library to come up with this stack. Six books, all of them about serial killers and murderers. Ed wondered if the librarians would add his name to some list they kept behind the counter. Serial killer junkies. Murder geeks. Or maybe Hannibal Lecter wanna-bes.

It was possible they even suspected that he was the Gentleman. But Ed doubted that. Sometimes being in a wheelchair was a weird kind of being invisible—no one ever looked at the wheelchair guy as a threat.

Ed grabbed the first book off the stack and flipped open the pages to the introduction. Staring back at him was a wild face framed by wilder hair. It was a woodcut picture of a killer from the Middle Ages—a man who had killed dozens of children near a small village in France. In the picture the man held a child in one hand. Not all of a child. Part of the body had already been eaten.

A quick flip of the page and Ed was facing newspaper sketches of a shadowy Jack the Ripper stalking the streets of Whitechapel in a cape and top hat. Across from the sketch was a diagram of a woman who had been dissected more completely than Ed's frog in freshman biology.

Another page and there was a black-and-white photo from the 1930s. This time the killer was a calm-looking man from Germany who had ground some of his neighbors into sausages. Flip.

He was looking into the fantastically mad eyes of Charles Manson.

On the next was the dumpy face of John Wayne Gacey.

Flip. Jeffrey Dahmer.

Flip. A middle-aged Russian guy with thick-framed glasses. Maybe he had killed fifty. Maybe it was a hundred. No one knew for sure.

Ed tried to read more of the text around the pictures, but he was having a hard time concentrating. And for an admittedly frivolous reason, when he considered the subject matter in front of him.

Gaia had a date. Ed's chance had been there. All he'd had to do was roll up to Gaia, open his mouth, and tell her how he felt. She had been right there. Right there.

Of course, she could have shot him down. Absolutely *would* have shot him down in flames. A girl like Gaia. Ed had to be crazy to think he could ever be more than friends with Gaia. He should be glad she even noticed him.

Ed looked down at his book and stared into the face of the Russian killer. A world that could put Ed in a wheelchair and have Gaia making a date exactly at the wrong moment seemed like just the kind of world that could produce a serial killer. They were probably as common as cockroaches.

The phone rang.

Ed stared at it with mixed emotions. It was a little early, but he had no doubt that it was Gaia on the other end. Usually, he called her, but since she was going to be out patrolling, and he was going to be fact-finding, she'd said she'd call him when she got in.

On most nights Ed looked forward to the late-night Gaia call. She was never exactly a blabbermouth, but compared to the way she was at school, Gaia was far more open on the phone. The phone calls were the only times when she really spilled her thoughts. Ed loved it. He just wasn't sure he could take it right now. Not after everything that had happened. He didn't think he could sit there and make happy noises while Gaia talked about her upcoming date. The thought made his blood curdle.

Who was this date-worthy guy, anyway? Where had he come from? And what gave him the right to ask out Perfection Personified?

The phone rang again. If Ed didn't answer, he wouldn't have to hear about the mystery guy. He wouldn't have to kick himself for being such a gutless wonder.

Of course, if he stopped answering, Gaia might never call again.

Ed scrambled for the phone.

"Hey," he said as he lifted the receiver, "I know why they call him the Gentleman."

"Is this Ed Fargo?" said a voice on the other end of the line. A guy's voice.

Ed stared at the handset in confusion. "Who is this?"

"Sam Moon," said the voice. "I'm trying to reach Ed."

Sam Moon.

Ed knew who Sam was. They had even spoken a time or two, but that certainly didn't make them friends. Back in the days when Ed had traveled sans wheelchair, Heather had been his girlfriend. Now she was Sam's.

"What do you want?" Ed's voice came out a little rougher than he had intended.

"It's about Gaia Moore," said Sam.

Wonderful. Did Sam have a date with her, too? Maybe she'd lined up the football team for the weekend. Open wound. Salt at the ready. "What about Gaia?"

"It's just that . . . well—"

Ed wasn't breathing. "Well, what?"

"You're her friend, right? I've seen you together."

"I'm her friend," Ed agreed. And that was probably all he was ever going to be. Once again tiredness and anger got the better of him. Still, it was nice that Sam had noticed. Maybe he was even jealous. "If you're looking for tips on asking her out, you better talk to someone else because—"

"I'm not calling about anything like that," Sam said quickly.

"Then what do you want?"

Sam took a deep breath.

"I want you to help me save Gaia's life."

"ARE YOU AWAKE?"

Quite Contrary

Gaia looked up. Or tried to look up. All she could see was dark and slightly less dark. Neither one of them seemed to form any shape that made sense.

"Don't worry," said a voice from the not so dark. A girl's voice. "I'm going to go call an ambulance."

"Uhh," Gaia grunted. She struggled to move her rigid jaw muscles. "Nuhhh."

No. Don't do that.

"Do you want me to stay with you?"

What Gaia wanted was for this disembodied voice to go away and leave her alone so that she could recover.

It was the most irritating thing—the real price of stressing her body in ways that no human being was built to take. For a few seconds, at most a few minutes, Gaia could push herself way past the limits of normal human strength and endurance, but when that time limit was up, Gaia's body went on strike. Her muscles stopped talking to her brain, and her body stopped moving. It would pass soon enough, but until it did, Gaia was absolutely helpless.

It was a feeling she didn't cherish.

"Look," said the voice. "I don't know what's wrong with you, but I don't think you're dying."

Great diagnosis, Doc.

"So I'm going to sit here with you and make sure you're okay." Gaia felt a warm body next to her arm. It didn't feel all bad, but she didn't want it there. "If you're not, I guess I better call an ambulance."

"Gooo way," Gaia managed to whisper. Gradually her muscles were waking up again, but she was still embarrassingly weak. She could probably get up; she just didn't want to try it in front of this girl.

Just how long had she chased the man in the black coat? Had they run two miles? Three miles? More than that? Every second of the run had been at a dead sprint. Add in a badly bruised knee and a shoulder that just might be dislocated, and Gaia felt like crap. Tired, abused crap.

Finally Gaia pushed her scraped hands onto the pavement and stood up shakily. She'd only been out for seconds, but it felt like an eternity to her.

"I think you really are going to live," said the girl.

Gaia licked her lips. "You sound surprised," she said in a harsh voice.

The girl shrugged. "Well, I've seen a lot of things, but I've never seen anybody kick ass one second and go into a coma the next. What are you on, anyway?"

Gaia started to laugh at the absurdity of the question, but it turned into a cough. A harsh, racking cough.

"You sure you don't want to go to the hospital?" the girl asked, reaching for Gaia's arm. "St. Vincent's is right down the street."

"No." Gaia shook her head. "I'll be all right. Really."

"Whatever you say," the girl said, eyeing her with disbelief.

Gaia turned her head and had to fight down a fresh wave of dizziness. "Where is he?"

"The guy who was after my purse?"

Gaia nodded.

"Don't know," said the girl. "He ran off. The way you hit him, I'd be surprised if he's not on his way to the nearest emergency room with a half-dozen cracked ribs."

All the systems in Gaia's body were coming back into action like a computer being booted up after a long sleep. Unfortunately, her nerves were waking up along with her muscles. There was pain everywhere.

Gaia thought she heard something behind her and turned quickly. Nothing was there, but the head rush that overtook her was so overpowering, she momentarily stumbled. The red-haired girl reached out for her.

"I've got . . . oof!" The slim girl stood in close and held Gaia with both arms. "Damn, girl. You're solid."

Solid. That was a nice way to say she weighed as much as a water buffalo.

"I'll be okay," she said. "Just go on. Let me sit here a little longer, and I'll be fine."

"Nope. If you're not going to let me take you to the hospital, you at least have to let me buy you a cup of coffee," the girl said. "Not that you need to add caffeine to whatever weird substance you've got running through your veins."

Gaia closed her eyes. "I don't think—"

The girl shook her head. "Come on. A double latte is the next best thing to surgery."

Gaia started to laugh, but it was still a bad idea. It made too many things hurt too much. Maybe sitting and sipping would be the best things for her right now. Besides, if Shadow Man came back, she couldn't be sure she could defend herself.

"All right," Gaia agreed. "Coffee."

HE WATCHED FROM THE BEST

Perfectly Pathetic

darkness he could find. Sweat poured down from his temples. His back. His underarms. His lungs felt like they'd been roasted over an open flame. Bent at the waist, holding his hands above his knees, he fought for breath. She was good. He had to give her that. But the scene in front of him made his pulse race faster than any sprint ever could.

She was also down. And she wasn't getting up. Couldn't, apparently. Not without help.

It was all he could do to keep from laughing through his gasps. How pathetic. How perfectly pathetic.

A skinny girl with tangly red hair was aiding the one. The target. The ultimate trophy.

His eyes narrowed into slits as his breath started to slow. He could take them both. Two for the price of one. He could practically smell them from here. The fear would smell even better. He licked his lips. He could almost taste it.

As the girls shuffled off, he straightened his back. There would be no satisfaction in taking her now. Not when she couldn't even walk on her own. The side dish wasn't enough to sweeten the deal.

He wanted a fight.

He would have what he wanted.

But there were too many cops around. Too many pissants. There would be no more girls in the park tonight.

Unless, of course, he dragged one there.

Once, when Gaia was a baby, she was playing in a sandbox in Central Park. It was a sunny day in early spring. I remember because Katia was picking buttercups and tickling Gaia's chin with them.

We turned our backs on Gaia for one moment. Just to clean up our picnic before retrieving her and heading for home.

Suddenly, out of nowhere, a crazed pit bull came charging at Gaia. She was two. Only two. Sweet. Small. Seemingly helpless.

Before I could blink, the pit bull was bearing down on Gaia and her playmate. With the attack instinct of an animal, my lovely daughter leaped at the wild dog and sank her baby teeth into the dog's hind leg.

That was when we knew we had a very special girl on our hands.

TOM MOORE

There was a
distinct
possibility **mary**
she could
like this
girl.

Sharing Stories

GAIA'S ARM WAS FLUNG AROUND THE red-haired girl's shoulders as they stumbled their way across the winding pathways. The muscles in Gaia's knee felt like they had been stomped flat, stripped raw, and rubbed in coarse salt.

They neared the entrance of the park and found a young policeman with an unlikely handlebar mustache standing guard over the end of the pathway. Gaia made an effort to stand up straighter, putting less of her weight on her smaller companion. The last thing she wanted was for the cop to think she was drunk or on some kind of drugs.

"What do you two think you're doing in there?" the policeman called as they approached.

"Just taking a walk," the red-haired girl said.

The cop gave a snort. "You picked a bad place for a walk. Didn't you hear what happened in the park last night?"

"They're only slicing up blonds," the girl replied. "It's in all the papers."

"I wouldn't be too sure about that." He paused and looked them over. "Besides, your . . . *friend* is about as blond as they come."

There was something about the way he said *friend* that caught Gaia's ear. Maybe it was because she was so tired, but it took her a moment to put the idea together.

Two girls. Walking alone. Arms around each other.

This guy thought they were lesbians.

Gaia leaned harder on her companion and smiled. Might as well give him a show. His already ruddy face darkened, and there was a spark of interest in his eyes.

Men. So predictable. He quickly glanced away.

"We're leaving the park now," Gaia said. "So we'll be okay."

When the policeman looked at them again, he seemed a little irritated. "Be careful," he said. "If you have to come back this way, go around the outside of the park."

"Sure," said the girl. "Thanks for the profound advice."

They moved away and turned down Sullivan Street toward a row of cafes. Tired as she was, Gaia watched the stream of people moving in and out of the buildings with interest. Living in the city that never slept certainly had its high points. Getting coffee and doughnuts at any hour of the day or night was civilization at its peak.

Now that there were other people around, Gaia thought again about her weakness. She pulled her arm away from the red-haired girl's shoulders. "I can make it on my own now."

"You sure?" The girl kept her arm at Gaia's waist for a few steps, as if measuring her steadiness, then let her go. "For someone who was unconscious five minutes ago, you've made a miraculous recovery."

"I heal fast," said Gaia.

"Let's hope so." The girl stopped by a narrow building with a red door and a long list of coffees displayed in the window. "Come on—I'm buying."

Inside, the place showed signs of being in the middle of a theme change. There was a blackboard over the counter that read Coffee Cannes and a big-screen TV stood in a corner playing some film with subtitles, but the framed movie posters had all been taken down and stacked in a corner. In the front half of the shop the tables had been removed along both walls, and even though it was after eleven at night, workmen were busily installing computers and workstations in their place.

The red-haired girl found a table as far from the chaos as possible—which wasn't very far—and dropped her slim body into a cane-bottomed chair.

"I'm going to stop coming to this place when they're finished with the remodeling," she said. "It was cool to get my coffee with a Bergman flick. Caffeine and data is not my mix."

Gaia carefully bent her swollen, tender knee and eased herself into a chair across from the girl. "You don't have to buy," she said. "I've got cash."

"Save it." The girl slid her purse from her shoulder and dropped it in the center of the table. "If it weren't for you, I wouldn't have any money to pay for this, anyway. The least I can do is buy you a cup."

Gaia looked up at the board above the counter. Coffee and milk appeared in every possible combination. "Coffee," she said. "Just coffee. Nothing fancy."

The red-haired girl grinned. "I know exactly what you need." She twisted in her seat and shouted to the man behind the counter. "Hey, Bill, bring two cups over here. And none of that weak-assed Colombian. Bring the *stuff*."

The man behind the counter gave a tired nod and turned to a row of gleaming steel machines. A few moments later he dropped two huge mugs on the table, then turned without a word and went back to his post.

The coffee in the mugs produced tall plumes of steam, but that didn't stop the red-haired girl from lifting her mug and taking a long gulp. She shivered as she lowered her coffee. "Ahhh, as long as there's coffee, life goes on."

Gaia took a tentative sip. It was strong, bitter, and blazingly hot. It also seemed to carry a caffeine kick that rivaled espresso. Gaia could almost feel the coffee circulating in her veins. Perfect.

The girl reached a small hand across the table. "I'm Mary," she said.

106

Gaia took the hand. "Gaia."

"Gaia." The girl squeezed her fingers for a moment before releasing them. "Cool. Like the goddess."

Gaia blinked. Was it just her, or were people around here getting smarter? "Hardly a goddess."

"Well, you were certainly a powerful force of nature tonight," said Mary. She lifted her cup and took another slug of hot coffee, then she planted her elbows on the table and looked at Gaia. "Wait a minute—I know you."

Gaia's shoulders tensed.

"You do?"

Mary nodded. "I saw you at a party. You were there with Ed Fargo." She stopped and grinned. "Heather Gannis went nuclear on your ass."

Gaia rolled her eyes. It figured. "Yeah, that was me."

"Cool," said Mary. "So, you know Ed?"

Gaia nodded. She suddenly felt even more self-conscious. Ed was one of the few people who had seen her in the middle of a postfight collapse. Pretty soon the two of them would be sharing stories.

"Uh," Gaia mumbled. "Can I ask a favor?"

"You don't have to ask," said Mary. She made a dramatic sweep of her hand. "As an ass-kicking goddess, anything you want is yours."

"Cool. I mean, okay." She took a breath. "Could you please not talk about what happened tonight?"

"Not even with Ed?"

"Especially not with Ed," said Gaia.

Mary looked disappointed. "Well, all right." A mischievous smile crossed her face. "It would make a hell of a good story, though. The way you hit that guy, I thought—" She shook her head. "I don't know what I thought."

Gaia took another careful sip of the hot brew and studied the girl across the table. She was tall, at least as tall as Gaia, ridiculously thin. But her features weren't "elegant." Mary had a short, narrow nose set above full lips. Her eyes seemed almost too large for her head and were colored an intense green, with hardly any traces or flecks of other colors. Her skin was pale and freckled, yet there was something exotic about the angle of her big eyes. But the feature that really caught the attention was the hair. Surrounding Mary's face and tumbling down her back was a tangled mass of curls, curls, and more curls. She kept pushing them out of her face, and they would bounce right back.

She was oddly beautiful.

"Where did you come from, anyway?" Mary asked. "What were you doing in the park?"

Chasing a supersonic serial killer.

"I was just out for a run," Gaia lied. "I heard you yell and thought maybe I could help."

Mary nodded, a smile on her lips. "You definitely helped. You probably saved my life."

"I didn't save your life."

"How do you know?"

Gaia shook her head. "That guy you were fighting was just an ancient hippie. He probably wanted some money for drugs."

"That guy was an ancient hippie with a *gun*," Mary said.

"Gun?" Gaia frowned and tried to think back. "I didn't see any gun."

"It was there," said Mary. "He had it in one hand and pulled on my purse with the other. I thought he was going to kill me."

"Why didn't you let go of the purse?" asked Gaia. She hated the question as soon as it was out of her mouth. People were always saying that. Sit still. Don't fight. Give the bad man your purse like a good victim.

"No one gets my purse," said Mary. "All my shit's in there." She stopped for a second, then lowered her voice. "Actually, I guess there's nothing in there that's worth dying for, but I was just pissed off. I hate not being able to walk across the park without someone bothering me."

Now that was a sentiment Gaia could fully agree with. "You really think that guy had broken ribs?"

Mary grinned broadly. "I sure hope so."

Gaia half smiled. There was a distinct possibility she could like this girl.

But she wasn't making any promises.

THE BLACK MERCEDES PULLED UP

behind a long line of police cars, the early morning sunlight glinting against their windshields. A few of the officers standing by gave it a glance, but no one moved to order the car away. Slowly the rear window rolled down.

Pile of Cattle

Loki looked out. It was ridiculous. Absolutely ridiculous. There had to be at least fifty policemen in the park. They were everywhere, from uniforms standing guard by the gate to technicians literally up in the trees.

Loki couldn't stop himself from laughing. It was all so silly. If there ever had been any clues in this place, this herd of cattle had destroyed them. Not that he expected the police to catch the killer. Not this killer.

Loki raised his window and pushed open the door. "I'm going to go over and take a closer look."

"Do you want me to come with you?" asked the woman in the front seat.

"No. Wait here. This shouldn't take long."

"Yes, sir," said the woman.

Loki climbed out and started toward the park.

A tall, African American officer blocked his way. "I'm sorry, sir. No one is admitted to the park this morning."

"Official business." Loki reached into the pocket of his overcoat and pulled out a badge case. He flipped open the case and held an FBI identification card up for the policeman to see. It was a fake, of course, but it was a very good fake. It came from the same machines that produced badges for actual FBI agents.

The officer looked from the card to Loki and back again. "Maybe I should get my lieutenant," he said uncertainly.

"There's no reason to do that," said Loki. "Just move out of my way."

The policeman stepped aside.

Loki moved on up the path. The day had started out overcast, and low clouds still blocked the rising sun, but as he approached the actual crime scene, Loki put on a pair of dark sunglasses. There were still a few men left in the NYPD who had once worked with him as a young government agent. It was many years in the past, and even that identity had been false, but in case any of those men happened to be on the murder investigation team, Loki didn't want to be part of an uncomfortable reunion.

The crime scene was in a grassy field near the corner of the park. A pleasant enough place, with benches, trees, and gray squirrels that dodged around the policemen's feet. Pleasant, but utterly boring.

Loki ignored several other policemen who tried to talk to him and walked straight to where the body lay crumpled on the ground. It was a young girl, as expected, with long blond hair splayed out in a fan around her head. There was blood matted into the hair. More blood on the ground.

"Can I help you?"

Loki looked around and saw a plainclothes officer. From the man's cheap coat and old-fashioned hat, he had to be a homicide detective.

"I'm Frank Lancino, Connecticut state police," Loki said. He reached into his coat and produced another identification card. Just as fake. Just as good. "I've been called in to consult on this one."

The detective nodded. "I heard they were talking to your guys." He jerked his head toward the body. "What do you think? Same asshole you had up your way?"

Loki knelt next to the body. The girl had been killed with a knife, but not with a single wound. There were cuts on the arms. Cuts on the legs. Puncture wounds that went all the way through the body and a long slice that cut halfway around her neck. "Yes," he said. "Yes, this certainly looks like the work of our boy."

The detective sighed. He jammed his hands into his tweed overcoat. "What are we going to do about this? Any ideas?"

Loki straightened. "First you need to talk to your

technicians." He pointed at the ground. "If they can't do a better job outlining a body than that, who knows what else they missed."

"That outline's not from this body."

"It's not?" Loki looked at the detective curiously.

"That's from the previous victim," said the detective. "It looks like the killer did this one on the same spot as the one from the night before."

Loki had to fight back a smile. It was a nice touch. A very nice touch. He squinted at the trees around them. What were the odds that the subject of this investigation was out there right now, watching them? Loki thought it was very likely. Every artist wants to see the reaction to his work.

"Can I ask you some questions about the cases you've seen?" asked the detective.

"Later," said Loki. "I need to get to the station house. I'm sure I'll see you there."

Loki quickly retraced his steps and retreated to the car. The woman hustled around to open his door for him, then jumped back behind the wheel to steer the big sedan away from the curb.

"It's going to be interesting," said Loki.

The woman's green eyes were reflected as she glanced at him in the rearview mirror. "When do you think they'll meet?"

"Soon." He glanced out the window at the passing scenery. Rushing pedestrians. Colorful awnings. A man hosing down the sidewalk. It was another world. "Even now they could be moving toward a meeting."

"And when they meet?"

Loki gave a quiet laugh. "It will be one unbelievable fight."

"What if she dies?" the woman asked, her voice tight.

"Well, then, she's failed," Loki said. If she couldn't handle this, she was of no use to him, anyway.

"She has more training," the woman said. "You've seen how she can fight."

"Yes," Loki agreed. "But he has another advantage. He knows what he is. He knows what he's capable of."

"What is he capable of?" asked the woman.

"Anything."

GAIA WOKE UP, THEN WISHED SHE
hadn't.

She rolled over and sat up in the bed with a groan. Even before she peeled back the covers, she had a good idea of what she was going to find, and the real thing didn't disappoint.

Dress for Distress

Her right leg was bruised from thigh to ankle. Her knee was one big scab, and every color of the bruised-and-abused rainbow decorated her leg—all the way from battered purple-blue to super-sickening yellow-green.

There was still a lingering whole-body soreness from her adventures the night before, but it wasn't as bad as she had predicted. Gaia was relieved to find that despite how awful her leg might look, it wasn't too stiff. She could walk without a problem, but it was going to be a while before she was up for another run like last night's.

She grabbed a pair of scuffed jeans from the back of a chair and carefully worked them up her injured leg. Then she pulled a hooded sweatshirt out of the closet and slipped it on. One glance in the mirror told the story. Gaia Moore, girl geek.

Why should today be any different from every other day?

She started toward the bedroom door, then had a startling thought. Today was different from every other day. Today she had a date.

Gaia groaned, limped back to the mirror, and took a longer look. She wasn't encouraged by what she saw.

Would there be time to change after school? Maybe. But what if David saw her in school? If he saw her like this, he would want to cancel.

Which would probably be a good thing. She

shouldn't have said she'd go out with him in the first place.

But that thought hadn't even made it across her brain before another one chased it.

What was wrong with going out with a guy? Couldn't she just allow herself to be normal for five seconds?

Gaia shook her head. It was too early in the morning to start arguing with herself. It was *always* too early to argue with herself. She half expected a little devil and angel to pop up on her arms and start debating.

"I'm going," she said aloud. "I'm going, and that's it."

"If you're talking about school," said a voice in the doorway, "then it's about time."

Gaia spun around and saw Ella standing in the doorway. As usual, Ella looked like she was dressed for an evening at the clubs. Even at eight in the morning the *über*-bitch looked ready for dancing. Or an affair. Probably whichever option presented itself first.

This morning her ensemble was a short, glossy leather skirt topped off by a green blouse with a neckline that showed the top of her breasts. Her scarlet hair was swept back from her face, worked into an elaborate coif that Gaia couldn't have reproduced given an entire week.

"Ever heard of knocking?" Gaia asked.

116

Ella arched one perfectly plucked eyebrow. "Not in my own house, I haven't." She waved a lacquered nail at Gaia. "What are you doing up here talking to yourself? School starts in ten minutes."

"Then I'm not late yet."

Ella gave a sigh that held all the exasperation in the world. "Just don't expect me to give you a ride. I have a business appointment this morning."

Gaia nodded. "Getting started a little early today, aren't we?"

The comment brought a frown to Ella's cherry red lips. "And what is that supposed to mean?"

"Nothing," said Gaia. "It's only that I noticed that you had a . . . business appointment last night, too. One that kept you out pretty late. Seems like you've had one every night since George went out of town."

Now Ella's lips pressed together so hard that Gaia was sure she'd have to reapply her lipstick. "Careful, Gaia." For a moment Ella looked almost dangerous. "George has done a lot for you. Your father meant the world to him. It would be ungrateful to insult his wife."

Gaia was about to make a reply to that when she noticed something odd about Ella's choice of words. "'Meant'?"

"Pardon?" Ella replied.

Gaia took a step toward her. "You said my father

117

meant something to George." Did Ella know something about him? Had something happened?

"Did I?" The sarcasm in Ella's voice was so acid, it could have eaten through steel.

Gaia was amazed to find that her throat was getting tight. She had trouble speaking. "Yes, you did." She was angry at herself. She'd shown Ella too much vulnerability.

Ella gave a sly smile that would do any cat proud. "Just a slip of the tongue, I'm sure." She turned away. A few seconds later, Gaia could hear the tapping of Ella's pointed heels down the stairway.

For several long moments after that, Gaia could only stand there, trying to catch her breath and get her thoughts under control. Her father had left her. He didn't care anything about her, so why should she care about him? Still, the tightness in her throat didn't want to leave.

"He's not dead," she told herself.

Ella was just trying to screw with her. That was all. Superbitch in action.

Gaia looked again at the girl in the mirror. Now she saw not only a beast with tree trunk legs and lumberjack shoulders, with tangled hair, dressed in tasteless clothes. Now the beast had bloodshot eyes, too.

There wasn't much Gaia could do about the legs or shoulders, at least not in ten minutes, but she could try to do something about the clothes. She stripped off the worn jeans as fast as she could without descab-bing her knee and tossed them on the bed. The sweatshirt followed. Then she confronted the dreaded closet.

The trouble with Gaia's wardrobe was that nothing inside the closet looked much better than the things she'd been wearing. Gaia had a pair of capri pants, but they did nothing but accentuate her she-hulk hips and legs. There were a few dresses wrapped up in dry-cleaner plastic. Gaia hadn't worn them in years.

Besides, any sort of skirt was out. Unless she wore it with jet black hose, the Technicolor glory of Gaia's bruised leg was bound to show. Even with black tights there was the possibility of blood and ooze and . . . nope. No skirt.

Gaia finally settled on a pair of drab olive draw-string pants. They weren't too attractive, but at least they were clean—and they hid her legs. Gaia fumbled through crumpled sweaters and sweatshirts before settling on a slightly less baggy black sweater.

She studied the results in the mirror. Lumberjack shoulders. Tree trunk legs. Tangled hair.

Unless the grunge look came back before first period, Gaia was as fashion-free as ever.

But serial
killers were
different.
They weren't
run-of-
the-mill **genuine**
killers **monsters**
who happened
to get away
with it more
than once.

ED HAD DONE STUPIDER THINGS

Odd Couple

in his life—most of them on a skateboard, surfboard, or other so-called extreme-sport implement, but this was high on his list of "I can't believe I'm doing this" moments.

He was skipping first period—cutting school—to see a guy who had stolen his old girlfriend. Worse than that, he was cooperating with a guy who obviously loved Gaia. Ed wasn't an idiot. Sam could spout that "oh I only want to help her" bullshit all day and into the next, but the truth was that Sam was seriously into Gaia. Worst of all, Ed knew that Gaia was seriously into Sam. The whole situation tied his intestines in knots. Big ones.

The assigned meeting place for their little get-together was the chess tables in the park—neutral ground. But the police still had the park closed off, so that spot was out. Instead Ed was patrolling the sidewalk along the north border, hoping to intercept Sam. And if he missed him, that was just too bad.

"Ed?"

Ed turned and saw Sam walking toward him. "What's wrong? Don't they have clocks in college? I was about to give up on you."

Instead of answering the question, Sam hooked his

thumb toward the park. "What's going on? Why the big crowd this morning?"

"Haven't you heard?" Ed asked, glancing at the organized mayhem. "The Gentleman made another call last night."

Sam's eyes flicked toward the trees at the edge of the park, and the tan went out of his square-jawed face. "You don't think . . . I mean, it couldn't have been . . ."

Ed seriously considered letting him stew for a moment, but his conscience got the better of him. "It wasn't Gaia."

"You're sure?"

"Yep," Ed said with a nod. "The TV guys say this one happened before eleven last night. I talked to Gaia after that."

Sam still looked concerned, but the concern was tainted by obvious envy. Score one for the Ed-man.

"Was she okay?" Sam asked.

"She was fine." Actually, the conversation had been disappointingly short. Gaia had said she was tired, and she hadn't wanted to talk about the murders. But Ed liked the idea that he knew more about Gaia than Sam did. Sam might be on Gaia's short list for sex, but Ed was the one Gaia talked to every night.

Sam fiddled with the collar of his oxford shirt. "Are the police any closer to catching this guy?"

Ed shrugged. "If they have any suspects, the papers aren't mentioning it. Except the *Post*—I think they've pinned it on Elvis, or aliens, or a coalition of brunettes jealous of all that fun blonds are supposed to have."

Sam only nodded. "I'm worried about Gaia."

That was the heart of the matter. That was what had convinced Ed to cut school and meet with a guy who he barely knew—but who he hated on general principle.

Sam was afraid because of how closely Gaia resembled the first girl killed in the park. For Sam it was about protecting a girl he feared was in danger.

For Ed it was a different story. Ed knew the big secret, and from the way Sam talked, he was pretty sure that Sam didn't. Sam apparently loved Gaia, but he didn't know that Gaia was Wonder Girl. He didn't know she could slice and dice Bruce Lee without breaking a sweat.

Ed was proud to be in on it. But it gave him more reason to be scared for her. Gaia wasn't just the killer's ideal victim; she was actively seeking the killer's attention. She was all set to find this demon, shove his teeth down his throat and his arms up his nether regions, then put in a call to the police. Case over. City saved.

It had seemed like a good idea. There wasn't much Gaia couldn't handle.

But Ed was no longer so sure. Between the phone call from Sam and his stack of serial killer bios, Ed worried that maybe Gaia was in over her head. Sure, she could land a roundhouse kick with the best of them. He had seen her take out three thugs in one go. But serial killers were different. They weren't run-of-the-mill killers who happened to get away with it more than once. These guys were strange, creepy. They were genuine monsters.

Ed was pretty sure that Gaia wasn't experienced in taking on monsters. When it came to these guys, she needed just as much help as the next person. Problem was, Gaia would never recognize the fact that she might need help—let alone admit it.

"What have you found out?" asked Sam.

Ed nodded toward a bench along the perimeter of the park. "Let's go over there where you can sit down," he said. "I'm tired of looking up at you."

Sam followed instructions. He went to the bench, sat, and waited for the Ed report.

"You know the basics, right?" Ed asked.

"Six victims," Sam started, then he turned his head and looked over his shoulder. "Seven now, I guess. Connecticut, New Jersey, and here. All of them stabbed, all of them blond, all of them around Gaia's age and size." He stopped and ran one hand through his ginger-colored hair. "That's about all I know. I don't even know why they call him the Gentleman."

"I do," said Ed. "It's from an old movie, *Gentlemen Prefer Blondes*."

Sam nodded slowly. "I've seen it. Marilyn Monroe, right?"

"Bingo."

Sam looked down at the ground and shook his head. "That's not much help. How are we going to catch this guy before he has a chance at Gaia?"

"We're not," Ed replied.

Sam's head jerked up sharply. "What do you mean?"

Ed rolled slowly back and forth in front of the bench. Wheelchair pacing. "You're the college guy. Isn't it obvious that if three states' worth of cops can't catch this guy, we're not going to do it?"

Sam's frown grew deeper. "Then why are we even talking?"

"Because," said Ed. "We don't have to find the killer." He raised one hand and pointed in the direction of the school. "We only have to stick to Gaia."

GAIA WAS THIRTY MINUTES LATE

Empty Chairs

to first period. Even compared to some of her previous arrival times, it was a new achievement in nonpunctuality. Even so, her teacher decided to ignore her.

125

Gaia had barely started at this school, and already she had been the butt of so many jokes, people were getting tired of it.

It was a good plan. Give them so much to laugh about that it wears them out. Too bad she hadn't actually *planned* to do it.

Gaia settled into her seat and the public address speakers crackled to life.

"May I have your attention, please?" said the voice of an unseen school office worker. "This is a school-wide announcement."

The last event deemed worthy of a schoolwide announcement had turned out to be a pep rally. Earth-shattering stuff.

"Due to recent events, the school will be closing early today. The last period will end at one P.M. Additional counselors will be on hand in the lunchroom for any students who feel they would benefit from a counseling session. School hours will return to normal tomorrow. Thank you." The voice ended with another squirt of static.

The announcement of an early end to the school day drew a few muted cheers but didn't get nearly the reaction that Gaia had expected. She leaned toward a skinny, red-haired guy at a nearby desk.

"What events are they talking about?" she asked. "Why let us out early?"

The redhead nodded his pointy chin toward a desk at the front of the room. An empty desk.

Gaia stared at the desk, trying to remember whose body normally filled it. It wasn't Hateful Heather. Heather was in her usual place of power at the center of the room. It wasn't Ed. Ed wasn't in this class. Gaia frowned as she tried to remember. It was . . . It was . . .

Cassie Greenman. The girl who had told Gaia about the killing the day before. The girl who had said they looked alike.

Gaia turned to the red-haired guy again. "What happened to Cassie?"

Redhead moved his lips to form a single word. Gaia didn't have to be much of a lip-reader to make it out. Gentleman.

The headache that had only threatened in Gaia's bedroom suddenly came on with full force. "Where?" she asked.

The guy looked toward the teacher and tried to avoid Gaia's attention.

"Where?" she said again, more than a little louder. "Where did it happen?"

"In the park at eleven o'clock," the redhead shot back. He picked up his book and opened it, angling the pages so they formed a screen to ward off Gaia.

It didn't matter. Gaia had asked all the questions that mattered. She closed her eyes and tried to fight back waves of nausea and confusion. It was too coincidental, too weird. Cassie knew about the murderer. Why in the world would she be any-where near the park at eleven o'clock at night?

How could Gaia have failed a second time? It almost felt like this killer was taunting her. Once again he had struck right under her nose. And this time it had been someone Gaia knew.

Gaia had thought she could catch this guy before he did any more damage. She had maybe hoped there was something good in being fearless. Maybe even something good in being a muscle-bound freak. Something that made her life worthwhile.

Obviously she was wrong.

I make friends pretty easily. I'm fun. I'm loud. I know how to have a good time.

People are drawn to me.

But I'm not always drawn to them.

But this Gaia person? I genuinely like her. She intrigues me. That's why I gave her my number and told her to call if she ever felt like hanging out.

It's obvious she never will, but it's a gesture. And when you make a gesture, sometimes people feel they owe you something. And when people feel they owe you something . . . Well, that can come in handy from time to time.

The sooner
the informa-
tion reached
Sam, the
better the
chance of
saving Gaia.

a
simple
job

TOM MOORE TUGGED DOWN ON

Murphy's Law

his brown cap and did his best to shade his face. He had no reason to suspect that anyone would recognize him on the campus of NYU, especially dressed as he was in the brown uniform of a package delivery-man, but it didn't pay to take chances.

Years of experience had taught Tom that Murphy's Law was always in full operation when you were un-dercover. If anything could go wrong, it would. Even when nothing could go wrong, it went wrong, anyway.

Today's expedition into the city seemed like a sim-ple thing—drop off a package, run, and hope that the person getting the package knew what to do with the information it contained. That only made Tom more cautious. It was the simple jobs that turned into nightmares.

He felt a little odd, walking between the square buildings along Washington Place. Part of it was the feeling that any older person gets visiting a college or high school. An out-of-place feeling. Only Tom didn't need to be surrounded by kids to feel out of place. He was out of place just being alive.

He reached the gray concrete steps of the dorm and hurried inside. Put on the right uniform, and you can get anywhere. Show a little paperwork, and people will even point out the right door.

Three minutes later, Tom had walked through a disheveled common room and was rapping his knuckles against a dented oak panel marked B4. He'd hand the boy the box and go.

A feeling of guilt added to Tom's uneasiness. This boy's relationship to Gaia had already led him into serious trouble. Involving him further might well get the boy killed.

Tom shoved away the guilt. He had to do what he could to protect Gaia. It would be impossible to get the information directly to her—Gaia was under almost constant observation. If Tom tried to get close, he would only get himself killed. And more to the point, Gaia as well.

There was no response to his knock. He tried again, rapping a little harder this time.

"Package," he called through the closed door. "Package for Sam Moon."

One of the doors on the other side of the common room opened, and an overweight young man, his hair shaved down to a dark stubble, stuck out his head.

"He's not here," he said, a strong southern accent in his voice. "I saw him leave about half an hour ago."

Tom frowned. "Do you know where he could be?"

The stubble-haired neighbor shook his head. "He

usually comes back here between classes. You want me to hold on to that for him?"

Tom's fingers instinctively tightened around the package. He ran through the possibilities. He could try to find Sam elsewhere. He had pulled the boy's class schedule off the Internet, and he could always wait for Sam outside a classroom. Unfortunately package delivery companies didn't usually ambush people in hallways.

He could try coming back later, but that had its own set of risks. The sooner the information reached Sam, the better the chance of saving Gaia.

Tom looked at the boy with the shaved head. There was no reason to think he couldn't be trusted. No reason except that he appeared to have about as many brain cells as a ceiling beam.

"If I give it to you, will you be able to give it to him today?" Tom asked.

"As soon as he shows up," the boy promised.

Tom hesitated a moment longer, then nodded. "Sign here," he said. He passed a clipboard over, watched the boy sign it, and then—reluctantly—handed him the box.

The boy stepped back and started to close the door.

Tom grabbed the edge of the door and held it open. "This is an important package," he said. "You need to see that he gets it right away."

"Yeah," the boy replied, obviously perplexed. "Sure." He pulled on the door, and Tom let it go.

"Tell him it's from Gaia," Tom said to the closing door. "An important package from Gaia."

The door closed with a click, and a moment after, Tom heard the sound of one, two, three locks being set. He stared at the old, scratched wood door for a moment, then turned and started out of the building.

He was aware that he hadn't acted like a deliveryman. It didn't matter. Sam's neighbor could think anything he liked.

As long as he delivered the package.

GAIA NEVER KNEW A PIECE OF
furniture could scream.

It was there in every class she had shared with Cassie Greenman. A desk. An empty desk.

Screaming Desk

It was just a plain desk, scratched up and written on by so many students, it was hard to even make out where one set of initials stopped and the next one started. A couple of pieces of plastic, some plywood, and twisted-up metal. But every time Gaia looked at

134

it, she heard this weird kind of wailing down deep in her brain.

She wondered if she was going crazy—even more crazy than usual. But Gaia didn't think she was the only one who heard the screaming.

All day, other people kept glancing over at the desk. The Empty Desk. And every time they looked that way, they'd get this expression on their faces. Instantly zoned. Even the teachers seemed to be looking at it as if they expected the desk to answer a question or make a comment on the class.

It was profoundly weird.

Gaia knew they cut a couple of hours off the day, but by the time the last bell rang, she would have sworn that she had been in school for at least three weeks.

If anybody had asked her what had been covered in her classes that day, Gaia couldn't have repeated a word. Not that she was ever Ms. Perfect Attention. But ever since the morning announcement the only sound track in Gaia's head was the screaming desk and a running loop of her conversation with Cassie.

As far as Gaia knew, it was the first time she had ever talked to Cassie. And the last.

The thing that really bugged Gaia, the thing she just could not get around, was this:

What in hell was Cassie Greenman doing in Washington Square Park at night? It didn't make any sense. Cassie had seemed genuinely scared of the killer. She had even talked about dyeing her hair to take her off the victim list. Cassie Greenman might not have been a rocket scientist, but anyone smart enough not to play on subway tracks would have known better than to go into the park.

Except Gaia, of course, but that was different.

Gaia took a last took at the screaming desk as she staggered out of class. It had eyeball magnetism, that desk. It was like a tooth missing right in the middle of someone's smile. You couldn't stop looking at it. Gaia wondered how long it would be before someone else sat there and filled in the gap. She was willing to bet that desk was going to be empty for a long time.

Gaia made it down the hall, pounded her locker into submission, and shoved her stuff inside.

Why hadn't she seen Cassie in the park? It wasn't exactly teeming with people. How could Gaia have missed her?

Thoughts of Cassie grew so thick, it was like walking around in a literal fog. Gaia trudged slowly along the hallway, lost to the world. Then she started around the corner by the school office and ran smack into what felt like a concrete wall.

She gave a mumbled "sorry" and started to move on.

"It's all right. At least this time you didn't knock me down."

Gaia looked up at the voice. "Huh?"

"Hi," said David. "Remember me? David Twain, boy obstacle."

Gaia blinked away the tangle of twisted thoughts. David hadn't felt like a wall yesterday. Last night must have taken more out of her than she thought. "What are you doing here?" she asked.

David grinned. "It's school. They make you go."

"I mean . . ." Except Gaia didn't know what she meant. Her brain was still deep in the Cassie zone, and she was having a hard time getting it back in the real-world dimension.

"I'm going to have to start wearing football pads," David said, rubbing at the back of his neck. Gaia watched his forearm where he'd rolled up his sleeve. He was better looking today. Somehow the thought pissed her off.

"Sorry," Gaia said again, stepping around him. "I'm not all here at the moment."

"Yeah, I've seen the studies," David said, shoving his hands in his pockets. His binder was tucked under his arm with one book. There was no backpack. Gaia brought her hand to her forehead, confused by her inadvertent observations. Since when was she interested in this kind of thing?

"What studies?" she asked, focusing in on the little space of skin between his dark eyebrows.

"About you," David replied. "Four out of five

doctors warn that you're a major source of bruises."

Gaia shook away the last of the Cassie fog and tried to concentrate on what David was saying. Some part of her brain told her that she had just missed a joke, but she was in no mood to go back and figure it out.

"Whatever." Another brilliant response from Ms. Gaia Moore, ladies and gentlemen.

David smiled. Dimples. Annoying.

"Well, *whatever* you are or aren't, I *was* looking for you," he said. "In fact, looking for you was my number-one objective for the afternoon."

"Why?" The fog was rolling back in.

"The date, remember?"

Gaia blinked. Date. For a moment the words belonged to a foreign language. Something they might say in the jungles of Borneo or maybe on the far side of the moon. Then she remembered. Coffee. Baklava. Her first ever genuine date. It was amazing what a little thing like murder could make you forget.

"Look, David," she said. "Maybe we shouldn't. You know, because of . . . Cassie and all."

His face was quickly overtaken by an expression of concern. "I'm sorry. Were you two close?"

"No. It's not that. It's . . ." Gaia wondered how David would react if she explained to him that she was the ugly sister of Xena, Warrior Princess, and

Cassie was one of the helpless peasants Gaia was supposed to protect from the rampaging hordes. "It bothers me."

David nodded. "It bothers me, too." He gave a quick look around the hallway. "I just moved here last week. Everybody keeps saying that New York is this really safe place, that there's not nearly as much crime as people say. They act like it's all in the movies. But I get here and there's this big murder thing going on."

Gaia shrugged. "They're only killing blond girls. You shouldn't have to worry."

That off-center smile crept back onto his face. "Yeah, but I kind of like blond girls," he said in a low voice. "I want to keep them around."

It wasn't the smoothest response in the world. On the Skippy scale, Gaia marked it closer to regular than extra creamy. But he was trying.

"Okay," she said. "Maybe we could go somewhere. Just for a little while."

"Anywhere you want," he replied. "If you don't feel like dessert, maybe we could just go over to Googie's and grab a burger."

Googie's. Yet another spot on Gaia's Guide to the Village. It was a place so tacky, it was . . . really tacky. "For a guy who's only been here a couple of days, you sure have homed in on prime sources of empty calories."

David patted his disgustingly flat stomach. "I have

a list of priorities whenever I move." He raised his hand and started ticking off the points. "First, locate an immediate source of sugar. Two, find a good greasy burger. Three, pin down a decent pizza." He lowered his hand. "Once all that's done, you're ready to move on to number four."

Gaia raised an eyebrow. "What's number four?"

The dimples retreated, and David looked at her for the first time with a completely serious expression. "Find the right girl to share it with."

Gaia had to give him credit. He was Not Sam, but he was good. She did a quick top-to-bottom survey. Chinos: pressed, but not too neat. Khaki shirt over black T-shirt: again, looking a little less than perfect. Just an average guy. And average was okay with her.

Gaia did a little mental arithmetic. If what she had heard was right, then both victims had died in the park in the middle part of the evening, somewhere before midnight. If Gaia was in place by nine-thirty, ten at the latest, she should be ready to tackle the killer if he came back for thirds—not that she would be the only person looking for him there tonight. She'd still have time for a quick dinner, a change of clothes, and working her way past Ella.

Not that the last part was hard. Ella had been off doing Ella things every night for a week.

"You're sure you want to go out with me?" Gaia

asked. She knew it was tempting fate, but she felt like she had to give him a final chance to back out.

David nodded. "Absolutely."

"Then here's the deal. Meet me at Third and Thompson at six, and we'll eat."

"What's at Third and Thompson?"

"Jimmy's Burrito." Gaia gave him her best excuse for a smile. "Even greasier than Googie's."

A Simple Plan

SAM LEANED AGAINST THE COOL STONE of the Washington Square Park arch. He looked around to make sure that no one was watching, then pulled a small yellow radio from his pocket and squeezed the trigger on its side. Even alone, he still felt like an idiot.

"Do you see her?" he asked. He let go of the trigger, then quickly pressed it again. "Over."

There was a moment of silence before Ed's voice came back. "Yes, I see her. I'm in a wheelchair. I'm not blind. Over."

"Which way is she going? Is she heading toward the park?"

Static.

"Ed? Is she going toward the park?"

Static.

"Ed?"

"You're supposed to say 'over' when you're done."

"Over, for God's sake. Is she going toward the park? Over," Sam snapped.

Static.

"Ed? I said over."

"I heard you. I was just moving to keep up with Gaia. Have you ever tried to roll and use a walkie-talkie at the same time?" he hissed. "Next time you decide to steal radios, I suggest you get one with a headset. Over."

Sam pushed the trigger again. "I didn't steal these. I paid for them."

It was at least temporarily true. They were good radios, guaranteed to have at least a two-mile range and fourteen channels, and they had fancy built-in scrambling so no one else could listen in on the conversation. Very nice radios. Also very expensive.

There was no way Sam could afford to keep them. So he had paid for them at an electronics store with a thirty-day return policy. As soon as Operation Protect Gaia was over, the radios were going back. At the moment they were paid for.

"Which way is Gaia going?" Sam asked again. "Over," he added quickly.

"It looks like she's going home," Ed's voice replied. "Probably to get ready for her date. Over."

Sam stared at the radio in his hand. He had to have heard that wrong. "Say again."

Static.

"Ed?"

"You didn't say 'over.' Over."

Sam squeezed the radio, envisioning Ed's neck between his fingers. "Can you forget the stupid 'over' and just repeat whatever it was you said?"

"I said, she's going home." There was a hint of laughter in Ed's radio voice.

Sam gripped the radio. "Not that part."

"Then what . . ." Static. "Oh, you mean the date."

"What date are you talking about?" It took all his effort to release the talk button so he could listen for a response he was sure he didn't really want to hear.

"Don't you know about the date?" More glee. Obvious this time.

Sam was glad there was at least a mile of space between them. If Ed had been close enough to reach, the Gentleman wouldn't be the only one in the park committing murder.

"Obviously I don't know about the date," Sam said slowly. "If I knew about the date, would I be asking about the date?"

"Gaia has a date tonight," Ed's voice replied. His

voice had changed. There was resignation in it now. "She warned me about it yesterday."

No one had warned Sam. Of course, Gaia and Sam weren't on the best of terms. They had basically no reason to speak at all. But Sam still felt blindsided by the enormity of Ed's announcement.

Gaia had a date. *She's not yours,* he reminded himself. *She was never yours.* Somehow he still felt betrayed.

"Who is she going out with?" Sam asked.

"A new guy," Ed replied flatly. "David something." Sam was about to ask another question, but before he could, Ed's voice came again. "I need to move again if I'm going to keep her in sight."

Sam pushed himself away from the cold marble of the arch. "All right. Call me if she comes back out. We'll work out positions."

"Roger," said Ed. "Over and out. Ten-four. Copy tha—"

Sam switched off the radio. He flicked a switch that would make it ring like a telephone if Ed called, then dropped it into his jacket pocket.

Sam went through a mental list of questions about the date, but he couldn't think of how to ask them without sounding jealous. Was he jealous? He thought about it for a moment and decided the answer was yes. He might not be able to define his own feelings about Gaia, but he was sure about one thing—he didn't want her going out with anyone else.

With Gaia gone back to her brownstone to prepare for the unthinkable date, Sam wasn't sure what to do. He could hang around the park for the afternoon, maybe get in a game. But losing a game of chess didn't seem very appealing without at least the chance of seeing Gaia.

After a few moments of indecision he turned to go back to his dorm. This was probably the only chance he was going to get to shower, eat something, maybe even grab a quick catnap. He would be back on duty soon enough.

Sam strolled across Washington Square North and headed uptown. The plan he and Ed had worked out was a simple one—until the Gentleman was caught, killed, or had moved on to another state, they would keep Gaia under close observation. Close observation defined as spying on her night and day.

There were two upsides to this plan. First, it would keep Sam occupied, thus keeping his mind off the obsessive kidnapping questions. Second, the plan involved seeing Gaia. A lot.

For today both Sam and Ed would both be on duty. If Gaia appeared, they would stay close. If Gaia got in trouble, they would help her. If they made it through the first day, they would switch over to working in shifts. Ed would watch Gaia during the school day; Sam would take over in the afternoons. It seemed like a simple plan.

Sam only hoped the killer was caught before Sam died from exhaustion.

A group of skateboarders went past, headed for the park, followed closely by a knot of laughing kids. The police had kept Washington Square locked up for most of the morning, but now that the barriers were down, the usual park population was rushing in to fill the void.

Sam cast a sideways glance as a barrel-chested man in a Greek fisherman's hat strolled past, a newspaper tucked under his arm. The man didn't seem familiar. He definitely wasn't a regular. Maybe he was the killer.

Another man went past. This one had a narrow, hatchet-shaped face and wild, bushy eyebrows. Killer material for sure.

There was a middle-aged Asian woman wearing a long, dark coat—an awfully heavy coat for a day that was pretty warm. She could have hidden anything under that coat. After all, even if the press called the killer the Gentleman, there had been no witnesses to the killings. Who was to say this Gentleman wasn't a Gentlewoman?

Sam was looking at another man when he realized how crazy this was. Of course these pedestrians didn't look familiar. Fifty thousand people must walk down Fifth Avenue to Washington Square on any day of the week. Maybe more like a hundred thousand. Sam couldn't possibly recognize them all.

It was time for Sam Moon to stop playing Sam Spade. A blast of sugar laced with caffeine, some sack time, and an icy shower were all required. Any order would do.

He managed to make it back to his dorm without spotting any more serial killer wanna-bes on the streets. But that didn't mean there wasn't still one out there. Maybe Sam could just have the caffeine and the shower. The nap would take too long. He couldn't leave Gaia out there alone while he snoozed. So no nap.

That decision made, Sam actually felt a tiny bit better. He walked through the common room and was about to open the door to his bedroom when he heard another door open.

"Hey, Sam," said a voice at his elbow. "Think fast."

Someone who had gone through high school playing basketball would have had an instant response to those words. Sam played chess. He turned around just in time to take a cardboard box between the eyes.

"Ouch," he said as the small package bounced off his forehead and thumped to the floor.

"You got bad hands, Moon." Sam's suite mate,

147

Mike Suarez, leaned back against his door frame, grinning.

Sam reached for the package. "My hands are okay; it's my head that's slow." He picked up the box and turned it over in his hands. "What's this?"

"Delivery guy brought it for you this morning," Mike replied. "That's all I know." He shrugged and winked. "You better work on those hands."

"Right." Sam returned the smile, although he felt more like smacking Mike's head right back.

Sam turned to the door and pushed it open, reminding himself for the umpteenth time that he really had to get that lock fixed. As soon as he was inside, he looked at the package again, wondering who might have sent it. It was a small box, little bigger than a stack of index cards, and the label had no return address.

There was only one way to find out. He grabbed the paper at the edge of the box and started to tug.

"Sam?"

This time the voice came from inside his room. Sam looked up in surprise and saw Heather sitting on the edge of his bed. "Heather! Jesus, you scared me."

Heather smiled at him. "We didn't have the best night last night," she said. "I thought I would try to make it up to you."

Sam opened his mouth to say something else, but

the subject slipped away before it could get to his tongue. Heather's long, rich brown hair had been set loose to spill around her shoulders. She was wearing a short, black skirt that ended well above her knees and a white shirt. A big white shirt.

"That's my shirt," he said.

Heather nodded. "I borrowed it." Her lips pursed into a pout. "I'm sorry. You want me to take it off?"

"No, I—"

The pout on Heather's lips was replaced by a sly smile. "I was hoping you would say yes." She raised her fingers to the top button and slowly slipped it open. Then she moved down to the next. "I think we should try again, Sam," she said. "The last time didn't end so well, did it?"

Her tone was inviting, but her eyes conveyed a whole other message. She was giving him a chance to make it up to her. Make up for chasing after Gaia and leaving her naked. Alone. Unsatisfied. One chance.

There was no way Sam was stupid enough to disappoint her. He didn't want to.

He quickly shoved the little package into his coat pocket next to the yellow plastic radio and closed the door.

Apparently there would be no nap, no shower, and no caffeine.

"Soon I'll be through the main course." He looked at Loki **stranger** over his shoulder. "I think I'll take up brunettes for dessert."

The Thing

"YOU MIGHT AS WELL COME OUT," Loki said calmly. "I know that you're following me."

The boy stepped out from the trees and stood in the dry grass at the edge of the sidewalk. "Well, if it isn't my dear uncle Loki," he said in a cheerful tone. "Whatever brings you here?"

Loki kept his hand in his pocket and closed his fingers around the comforting bulk of his 9-mm pistol. "You couldn't resist, could you?" he said. "You had to come and watch."

The boy shrugged. "I admit, there is a certain pleasure in watching all the little bugs scurry around." He waved his hands extravagantly. "The police run here. The FBI runs there. And you run in between."

"Do you think this is funny?"

"Oh, very," the boy said. "But that's not why I'm here."

"Then why are you here?" Loki took a half step back. He tried to judge the odds. His skills with a firearm weren't as polished as they had been ten years before, but he was still quite fast. He could pull his semiautomatic pistol and get off ten rounds before most men even realized he had moved. But against this boy . . . Loki thought his chances of surviving were no better than fifty-fifty.

The boy turned and looked back through the

screen of trees at the people passing through the park.

"Actually," he said, "I was only taking in the menu. Picking out a little something for tonight." He gestured at a group of girls laughing near the fountain. "There are so many possibilities here."

Loki studied the boy as if he were a stranger. It was almost true. A year before, the boy had been just that—a boy. A boy with an unusual predilection. Then he'd been unsure of himself. Awkward. Looking to Loki and others for guidance.

A year could change everything. The man—the thing—that Loki faced had as little relation to that uncertain boy as a kitten did to a tiger. In every way that counted, he was a stranger.

"I didn't think any of that group would be to your taste," Loki replied, glancing at the gaggle of young women.

"No?"

"I thought you were only after blonds."

The stranger with a familiar face laughed. "So true," he said. "But that was only the appetizer. Soon I'll be through the main course." He looked at Loki over his shoulder. "I think I'll take up brunettes for dessert."

Loki frowned. He wasn't squeamish. He never had been. One life lost, a hundred lives lost, what did it matter? But there were things he cared about: years of work, research, effort. Those things should never be wasted.

Against his better judgment he took a step forward. "Come back," he said. He thought about touching the stranger's shoulder but decided against it. "Come home."

"Home?" The boy made a noise that might have been the start of laughter but quickly turned into something more like a growl. "Home," he said again. His face twisted into a sudden sneer, and he began to pace back and forth between the trees and the edge of the concrete path, his black coat billowing in the wind. "Couldn't you find a better word than *home?*"

"It was your home," Loki said in his most reassuring tone. "For most of your life you were—"

The boy whirled. His eyes were sharp. "Oh, don't say happy," he snapped. "It was an experiment. A rat cage. A prison. Not a home. And I was never, ever happy in that box." He raised his arm and pointed an accusing finger at Loki. "That place is the reason I'm here. The reason for everything."

Loki sighed. It was a sad, tired sound, the sound of an old man who was past his prime and weary of the world. It was a sound Loki had practiced.

"All right," he said. "I don't suppose there's anything I can say to make it better now." Hidden in the pocket of his coat, his hand tightened on the grip of the pistol. He began to raise the barrel.

The boy blinked, and as quickly as it had come, his

rage seemed to evaporate. A broad smile returned to his face.

"Don't tell me you're going to shoot me," he said. "Not after you've come so far to ask your poor prodigal son to come back to the farm."

For ten seconds they stood in silence. Loki had no idea what the boy was thinking, but his own mind was playing over scenarios as fast as a chess computer trying out moves. In this game there were only two opening moves: Leave the boy alone or kill him. Each of those moves had its possibilities and its dangers. Loki made a quick glance around and judged his distance from the other people in the park. There were no police nearby, and the risk of auxiliary damage was low. Now was the time.

"I was wrong to let you out," said Loki. "You're undisciplined. Unready. You have to come back with me."

"Or you'll kill me," said the boy.

Loki nodded. "Yes."

The boy was fast. Incredibly fast. One moment he was ten feet away. The next Loki's hand was hit by a rock-hard blow that sent the automatic pistol spinning away. Before he could react to that first attack, a fist cracked against his chin. He reeled backward, red fog swirling in his brain.

Strong hands caught Loki by the shoulders and spun him around.

"You made me the way I am for a purpose," the boy hissed in a low whisper, "but I've got my own objectives now. The first one is to kill your golden child." The fingers tightened. "And then I'm coming for you."

The boy released his grip, stepped back, and smiled. It was almost serene. He touched one finger to his forehead in a mock salute, then turned and strolled casually across the park.

Loki watched him go. In a way, he was greatly relieved that he hadn't managed to kill the boy. He couldn't be certain if it was the right decision.

But he would know soon enough.

A Happy Gaia

THE BEST THING ABOUT HAVING A date at Jimmy's was that it had all the ambiance of a shoe box. Maybe less.

That didn't mean Gaia didn't like it. Ambiance came way, way down on the list of her requirements in a restaurant. Way below sour cream and globs of melty cheese.

Besides, no ambiance equaled no need to dress up. No need to dress up equaled no need to worry about changing clothes. No need to worry about changing clothes equaled a happy Gaia.

That was the theory. In the real world she decided to make a change.

What she really needed was something dark. Something nice. Cool. Something sort of *Matrix-like*. Something that would hide stains.

Fat chance of finding it in her closet. This was depressing. For a split second Gaia thought of the red-haired girl. Mary. The smudged number on the crumpled coffeehouse napkin in the pocket of last night's jeans. Had Mary meant it when she said to call her? Was that what girls did? Call for advice before dates?

Right. Like that was going to happen.

Gaia went back to the black jeans she had looked at in the morning and decided to give them another try. They fit a little snug—snugger than she would have liked across her bulging butt. Still, they didn't look too bad.

She stared a few minutes longer, then closed her eyes, reached in, and selected a hanger at random. Gaia opened her eyes to peek. A big denim shirt. Not an inspired choice, but at least a choice.

She gave her hair a few strokes, pulled it back, and slipped it through her one and only scrunchie. There. She was dressed, and the whole thing had taken less than half an hour. It had to be a new record.

Gaia checked the clock. Plenty of time to cruise by the park, lose a game to Zolov, and still be early for her date.

Date.

Gaia felt a shimmery feeling in her legs. Not a major quake, but at least a 3.5 on the `do-I-really-want-to-go-through-with-this scale`. The date was only a couple of hours away, and she still couldn't get a good handle on the idea. Gaia was going to a restaurant. With a guy.

It wasn't a completely unknown situation. She had been out on social occasions before. Of course, the last time was probably when she was twelve. It wasn't completely unheard of. Except this time the guy was actually coming because of Gaia. He would look at Gaia. And talk to Gaia. Worse, he would expect Gaia to talk back and `be interesting` for minutes on end.

She wondered if she could just keep her mouth full of burrito and let him talk. Guys liked to talk. That's what she had heard, anyway.

With this stellar plan in place Gaia started downstairs, sure that she was on her way to end her status as the world's oldest undated girl. It was possible that she would even break the great `kiss curse`.

But a new obstacle was waiting for Gaia before she reached the ground floor. She closed her eyes and sighed.

157

She'd forgotten about the Wicked Witch of the Wonderbra.

Ella looked at Gaia over the rims of her purple-tinted sunglasses. "Where are you going?"

"Nowhere," Gaia replied.

Ella smirked. "Then maybe you shouldn't go. It's getting late."

"Late?" Gaia pointed at the window beside the staircase. "It's barely after four. It's broad daylight out there."

Ella pursed her glossy lips. "I know, but with all those murders going on, I really think you need to stay in. It's just too dangerous."

The person on the stairs looked like Ella. The perfume drifting toward Gaia in invisible clouds certainly smelled like Ella. But her mind had clearly been replaced by the mind of someone else—someone who cared if Gaia kept breathing.

Or at least bothered to pretend to care.

What the hell was she supposed to say? Part of her just wanted to walk out like she normally would, but some morbid part of her was tempted to play along.

"I . . . uh . . . won't stay late." That was at least partially true. Gaia could circle back by the brownstone after her early date with David. Then she could slip out again as soon as Ella got over this caring fit.

Ella waited a few seconds, then nodded. "All right," she said, "but whatever you do, stay out of the park.

And try to get home before eight. It's a school night."

Gaia stared. Body snatchers were definitely at work. This whole conversation could not be occurring. Not with Ella.

She tried to answer but could only manage a nod. Ella's behavior had baffled Gaia beyond the ability for rational speech.

SAM WONDERED IF YOU COULD

Timing Is Everything

drown in hair. Heather's hair was long and lush and altogether beautiful to look at. Breathing through it was a different story. No matter how Sam turned in the narrow bed, he seemed to end up with a suffocating curtain of brown spilling over his face.

Heather murmured something and snuggled against him. Her soft skin felt extraordinarily warm against his legs and chest.

Like Heather, Sam was nearly unconscious in a postsex daze. It was amazing. Sex was like the greatest sleeping aid in history. One minute he was more charged up than he had ever been in his life, the next minute his arms and legs seemed to weigh a thousand tons. Each.

Sam pushed open a gap in Heather's hair wide enough to permit a breath of air. He couldn't allow himself to actually sleep. With the serial killer working the neighborhood, Heather's parents would panic if she was out late. And Sam had something to do. Something important. But for the moment he couldn't remember exactly what it was. He settled himself against Heather's warm softness and began to slide toward sleep.

This wasn't so bad. He could live with this. Having a beautiful girl naked in your bed was about as close to perfect as life could get.

For the moment, at least, Sam's obsession with Gaia seemed distant. Silly. There was nothing wrong with Heather. So what if she didn't know what a rook was? So what if she had a small cruel streak? It would be okay. It would work out. He was sure that he could love Heather.

Except, as his drowsiness pulled him down the slope toward true sleep, he brushed his lips against Heather's brown hair and imagined it was gold.

A buzzing alarm began to sound. Sam groaned and flapped his arm at the clock on the bedside table. He smacked the button over and over, but the noise kept coming.

"Mmmm." Heather rolled over and brushed her

lips against his face. "Turn that off," she whispered.

"I'm trying." Sam propped himself up on one elbow and picked up the clock. He pressed the button again. He slid the alarm switch to off, but the noise didn't stop. He stared at the clock blankly for a few seconds longer, then realized what was wrong.

The sound wasn't coming from the clock.

Sam scanned the room, searching for the source of the noise. It wasn't the phone. It wasn't the stereo. It was . . . a coat.

Across the room Sam's jacket was lying folded across the back of a chair—not the neatest fold in the world, but then, he had been in sort of a hurry to get undressed. For some reason, the coat was buzzing.

"Sam," Heather called. "Please. That's so annoying."

"Sure. Right." Still more than half asleep, Sam carefully eased himself away from Heather and rolled off the side of the bed. He stumbled over discarded clothing, banged his knee against his desk, knocked over a stack of books, and made it to the coat without generating any more noise than a rogue elephant in a bell factory. He fumbled in the pocket of the coat and grabbed something. What he pulled out was a bright yellow plastic radio.

Sam's heartbeat slammed to a stop.

Oh, yeah. The radio.

Free of the coat, the buzzing noise was louder than ever. Sam flipped the radio over and over in his hands, searching for the switch. At last he located the trigger on the side and pressed it. The buzzing stopped.

Sam breathed a low sigh of relief. He would call Ed back as soon as he could, but in the meantime at least the radio was quiet. The last thing he wanted to do was explain to Heather what he—

"Sam?" said a loud voice from the radio. "Sam, are you there?"

Panic shot through Sam. All remains of the after-sex sleepiness were blown away in an instant. He looked at the bed, trying to ascertain whether Heather was waking up, then he squeezed the trigger on the radio.

"I'm here," he said as softly as he could.

"Took you long enough," Ed's voice replied. "I've been sitting here buzzing you for the last five minutes. I was about to give up."

Sam wished he had.

Heather rolled over on the bed and stretched her hands above her head. "Sam," she said in a voice that was half a yawn. "Who's on the phone?"

"Nobody important," Sam replied with forced cheerfulness. "Go back to sleep." He lowered his voice and spoke into the radio. "Look, can you call me back later?"

"Hey, this thing was your idea." The quality of the radio was plenty good enough to pick up the irritation in Ed's voice. "Are you going to help me or not?"

"What's happening?"

"She's in the park," Ed answered. "She's been playing chess against that old guy. The Russian."

"Zolov," said Sam. "He's Ukrainian."

"Whatever. The game's over, and she's leaving."

Heather raised her head and rubbed at her eyes. "Sam . . ."

"Just a minute." Sam walked across the small room and stood as far from Heather as he could. "Look, can't you follow her?" he whispered to the radio.

"I'm too obvious," Ed replied through a crackle of static. "If I leave the park, she's going to see me."

Sam sighed and closed his eyes. They should just let her go. This whole business was seriously screwed up.

Sam squeezed the trigger, ready to tell Ed to pack it in.

For a full five seconds Sam held down the little button, but the words wouldn't come. If he gave up and something happened to Gaia, Sam would never be able to live with himself. That much he knew.

"All right," he said in a low tone. "Watch her as long as you can. I'll be right there."

"Hurry."

Suddenly Sam noticed a small plastic switch at the top of the radio. He flicked it, and the speaker inside went dead.

He'd found the off switch. Great timing.

Heather sat up and held the white sheets against her chest. "What's wrong?" she asked.

"Um, nothing," Sam said. He moved across the darkened room and found his clothes lying on the floor. Still trying to be as quiet as he could, he picked up his pants and began to slide them on.

"Where are you going?" asked Heather. There was a lingering fog of sleep in her voice, but it didn't hide an edge of irritation. "Aren't you going to stay with me?"

Sam ran a hundred excuses through his mind, but all of them seemed too lame to speak.

He could always tell her the truth. On the other hand, he wasn't ready to die.

"I have a class," he said.

"Now?" Heather pushed her hair back from her face and frowned at him. "I thought you had a short day on Tuesdays."

"It's a lab," Sam replied. He dragged out his shirt and began to put it on as fast as he could. "A . . . um, makeup lab from one I missed earlier."

"How long will it take?"

That depends on Gaia.

"A couple of hours," he said. "Three at the most." He finished with his shirt, dropped into a chair, and started putting on his shoes.

Heather stretched her long, bare legs but didn't get up. "Then I guess I better get dressed, too. I have to get home."

"Okay," said Sam. He stood up. "I've got to run, or I'll be late."

Heather pulled the pillows together and leaned back against them. "All right," she said. "Mind if I use your shower before I go?"

Sam smiled. "No problem. I wish I could stay."

He did wish he could stay. Although the decision to watch over Gaia was already made, Sam felt a fresh wave of indecision.

After all, the last time he'd left Heather to chase Gaia, he'd ended up kidnapped and half dead.

It would be nice if he could stay here. It would be nice if he could think of nothing but Heather.

It would probably be a lot safer, too.

But the undefined feelings he had for Gaia Moore were too hard to ignore.

Sam picked up his jacket and put it on. As he did, he noticed the small package still nestled in the right-hand pocket. He took out the box and held it up to the light. Small box. Brown paper. Nothing special. He started to leave the package behind, then he changed his mind and dropped it back into the

165

pocket. If he ended up on a nightlong Gaia stakeout, he would at least have something to look at.

"Well, I guess I'm going," he said as he moved toward the door. "Are you going to be all right going home by yourself?"

"I'll be fine."

There was a new tension in Heather's voice that caught Sam's attention. He turned back to her and looked at her lovely face. "Are you sure?"

"I'm sure," said Heather.

Sam wanted to ask her more, but Ed was waiting and Gaia was moving. If he was going to catch up to them, he needed to get outside. "Okay, then, bye."

He turned and grabbed the doorknob. He was halfway into the hall when Heather called again.

"Sam?"

"Yes?" he replied without turning.

"Does this have anything to do with her?"

Heather named no names, but Sam didn't bother to ask for a definition of "her."

"No," he said in a hoarse voice. He cleared his throat and tried again. "No, it's just class."

He waited a few seconds more, but Heather said nothing else. Sam stepped through the open door and left.

"I fear nothing," David said. "That's another of my special powers."

david

AT FIRST GAIA WAS FEELING FAIRLY
pleased with herself. She was
handling this date thing okay.
No pressure. She had even kept
it together in her game against
Zolov. She'd lost, of course, but
she always lost to Zolov. At least
this time she had come close.

The Wild Burrito

She tugged at the scrunchie in her hair as she
walked. There was absolutely no reason to get tense
about this dinner. They were only going to grab fast
food from a cheap restaurant. Nothing fancy.

She was fine—right up until she turned the corner
onto Thompson. The closer Gaia got to Jimmy's, the
more she could feel a pressure pushing her backward.
It was as if there were this weird wind coming from
the restaurant. It blew harder as Gaia got closer until
every step toward the restaurant was like pushing into
a gale. Other people walked down the sidewalk with
no trouble, but Gaia felt like any moment the wind
might grab her and send her flying back across the
park.

Gaia slowed. Jimmy's Burrito was only a dozen
steps away, but they were hard steps to take. She
steeled herself, squared her shoulders, and walked to
the door.

Lightning didn't strike. No earth-
quakes shook the ground.

Gaia took a deep breath. She glanced inside, scanned the tables and booths. No sign of David.

Maybe he wasn't coming.

David had probably wised up at the last moment. Maybe he had talked to someone else at school. Maybe he had finally come to his senses. Whatever the case, it was clear he had realized that dating Gaia was a big mistake.

Disappointment settled into Gaia's empty stomach like lead, but there was an equal amount of relief. No David. No date. There was still some chance of potential irritation if the story "How Gaia Got Stood Up" became part of the next day's grind of boring school gossip. But Gaia doubted that would happen. The story was too dull, considering what was going on.

"So what do you recommend?" a voice asked.

Gaia turned to find herself face-to-face with David. She struggled for something witty to say, but her well of wit was experiencing a drought. "I, um . . . I see you found the place."

David tapped a finger against the tip of his nose. "Able to detect taco sauce at a hundred paces." He held up his arms and pretended to flex huge muscles. "It's one of my secret powers."

Gaia forced a smile. She actually *wanted* to smile, but her face wasn't responding to her brain, so she had to force it. "You have others?"

"Too many to number," David said. He crowded in close to Gaia and leaned forward to look at the menu taped up against the window. "What's good here?"

"Depends on what you think is good." He was very much in her personal space. Gaia stepped aside, hoping it wasn't the wrong thing to do. He didn't even blink.

"Anything," he said. "As long as it's hot."

"They have plenty of hot," Gaia said. Another smile. This one didn't take as much effort.

"I am the terror of hot peppers everywhere." David stepped past Gaia and pulled open the front door. "Jalapeño parents tell stories of me to frighten their children."

This time Gaia actually laughed. Suddenly all the tension she had felt about this date seemed completely stupid. David was just a person. A funny person who, for some reason, seemed to like her. None of those things was bad. Not everything she did had to turn into a disaster movie. Did it?

She stepped through the open door and waited for David to follow. "I'm not talking about wimpy peppers like a jalapeño," she said as he entered.

"Jalapeños are wimpy?"

"Extremely," she said. She was bantering. This was banter. Who knew?

They walked past the newsstands inside the door. Gaia picked out a booth off to the side of the restaurant and slid her butt across the red vinyl seat.

"They serve serious peppers here," she said. "They don't mess around."

David dropped into the seat across from her and pulled a plastic-coated menu from between two bottles of hot sauce.

"So what makes a serious pepper?" he asked. "I'm ready to do battle with any vegetable in the place."

"Good." Gaia reached across the table and plucked the menu from his hand. "Then I'll order for us."

"Go ahead," said David. "I'm not afraid."

Gaia looked at his blue eyes. Something weird was going on. She actually felt, well, almost comfortable. This was not her. This was some other girl who actually knew how to talk to other human beings.

A waitress approached, and Gaia delivered the order. David picked up the menu again after the waitress left. "What's the special burrito?" he asked.

Gaia snatched the menu a second time. "Just a burrito."

David's eyes sparkled. "But what's so special about it?"

"You'll see," said Gaia.

Much to her own surprise, Gaia was actually enjoying herself. So far, at least, she hadn't suffered from a brain fart causing her to say something inexcusably stupid. It was only a matter of time, of course, before she was revealed as a hopeless social outcast, but at least she was enjoying a few moments of normal life.

"So . . . ," David said.

Gaia stared at him. "So . . ."

They lapsed into silence. Uh-oh. This was getting less good. Gaia pressed her hands against the sticky vinyl. Was she supposed to say something? Was *he* supposed to say something?

That was when the emergency cop-out system flipped into action. Gaia stood up, nicking the edge of the table with her bad knee.

Ow.

"Where are you going?" David asked.

Gaia took a deep breath. "Bathroom."

"SO YOU'VE PROVED YOU'RE AN IDIOT

with nothing to say," Gaia told her dripping reflection. The cold-water-in-the-face splash had done nothing for her spirits. It had only served to form huge blotches on her shirt and soak the hair around her face. Lovely.

Not Quite Normal

She might as well go back out there and seal the deal. Send him running for the hills. If the city had any.

Gaia opened the door and was headed back down the dark, grimy hall past the kitchen when she heard a huge crash, followed by a bloodcurdling scream. She stopped in front of the open kitchen door.

There was a fire. A big one.

This could really put a damper on her already dampered date.

Without hesitation Gaia strolled into the kitchen, took the phone out of the hand of a trembling fry cook, and hung it up before he could dial 911. She grabbed the fire extinguisher and yanked it off the wall, walked over to the searing, leaping flames, and doused them with one good squirt.

The sprinkler system didn't even have time to kick in.

Gaia turned and looked at the three white-clad, grease-stained kitchen workers who were huddled in the corner, looking like they'd fallen there out of shock. From the way they were gaping at her, she could have been an angel plunked in the middle of their crusty linoleum floor directly by the hand of God.

Gaia flushed. Sometimes she forgot her reactions to danger weren't quite normal.

She took a deep breath and tried to smile. "Uh . . . you can still make the burritos, right?"

"EVERYTHING OKAY BACK THERE?"
David's face wore a worried expression as Gaia returned to her seat.

Family Stuff

"Fine," she said, averting her eyes. She cleared her throat noisily. "And dinner is on the house."

He glanced past her toward the kitchen, a question obviously forming. "Why did they—"

"So how do you like New York?" she interrupted, placing her hands flat on the table. Lame question. Better than trying to deal with his.

He narrowed his eyes at her, obviously mulling his options. Which line of questioning was better/safer/more intriguing? Finally he leaned back into his bench, resting one arm across the top.

"I'm not sure yet if I like it," he said.

Gaia smiled, glad he'd made the right choice.

He looked toward the windows at the front of the restaurant. "It's great to get a burger anytime you want," he continued, "and to find an open bookstore at three A.M., but I think it's just too crowded for me."

"I like crowds," Gaia said, watching a group of people standing in line to pay their bill. "It's easy to get lost in them. Go unnoticed."

She felt her skin flush. She stared at the chipped tabletop. She hadn't just said that, had she?

174

"I can't imagine you'd go unnoticed anywhere," David said.

Gaia blushed more deeply. He hadn't just said that, had he?

"Anyway, I don't know if I'll be here long enough to adapt," David said.

Gaia glanced up. "You just got here. Why would you be moving?" Why wouldn't he be moving? She'd waited seventeen years for a first date. She'd probably be waiting another seventeen for a second.

"You know." David shrugged. "Family stuff." For the first time he looked a little uncomfortable.

"Following your parents' jobs?"

Now David looked down at the table. "My parents are . . . I'm not with my parents."

Gaia felt a nearly irresistible urge to touch him. "That's something we have in common," she said. "My parents are gone, too."

David raised his head. "That's weird, isn't it?"

For a moment they just looked at each other. This silence wasn't nearly as uncomfortable as the first.

"What is this?" David asked.

"What?" Gaia asked back.

David pointed up. "This music," he said.

A song played from invisible speakers. Gaia hadn't noticed it until that moment. She strained to hear.

175

Her waiting dark heart,
The violence in her eyes,
The hunger in my body,
The things she denies.

"It's this band called Fearless," Gaia replied, shaking her head slightly. "They play around here."

"Fearless?" David repeated, raising his eyebrows.

Gaia confirmed with a nod. At one point when she'd first moved to New York, it had seemed like this random band with this ironically appropriate name was following her around. It was almost too bizarre. But now it didn't even affect her. She was used to it.

The waitress came back with two oval platters loaded with burritos, corn flour tacos, and heaps of seasoned rice and beans. Gaia took her plate and dug in quickly, sweeping together a blob of sour cream, rice, and a chunk of steaming burritos. The combination of flavors was almost too good.

David eyed his plate. "What are all these little brown peppers?"

"Ever heard of *habañeros?*" Gaia asked through a mouthful of food.

His eyebrows scrunched together. "I don't think so."

Gaia grinned at him. "Good luck."

David picked up one of the peppers between his fingers, examined it for a moment, then tossed it into his mouth. Gaia heard it crunch between his teeth. A moment later David's blue eyes opened so wide, they looked like they might fall out of their sockets.

"Wow," he whispered.

"Pretty hot?" asked Gaia.

He nodded. "I don't think I'm really tasting it. It sort of made my ears ring."

Gaia took another bite of her own meal and watched as David chewed his way through a second pepper. "Most people are scared to death of those things."

David took a third pepper and crunched it. A red flush spread over his face, and he trembled.

"I fear nothing," David said. "That's another of my special powers."

Gaia looked at him. Maybe they had more in common than she thought.

SAM MOON WAS AN IDIOT.

The Other Guy

Nope. Even *idiot* didn't sound bad enough. It was an insult to idiots everywhere.

He had started out in situation A. In situation A he was lying in bed with a beautiful girl. A beautiful naked girl. A beautiful naked girl who wanted nothing more than to be with him. A girl with whom he had just had sex.

But from there Sam had proceeded straight to situation B. In this case he was up, out of bed, and running off to chase a different girl. Only this girl didn't want him. Probably hated him. Definitely didn't want to have sex with him.

Oh, yeah, and she was on a date with someone else.

As Sam crossed the street and stopped in the middle of the crowded sidewalk, he hoped his parents would someday have another son. He would be wrong ever to pass these pitiful genes along to the next generation.

Sam stood across from Jimmy's Burrito and watched Gaia eat her dinner with the guy she was dating. The back of the guy's head was nothing special. From what Sam could see, the pair were eating, talking, and even laughing.

Gaia was laughing.

Sam's heart squeezed. He tried to think of all the times he had been with her—which weren't many. Now that he thought about it, Sam wasn't sure he had ever gotten her to smile, much less laugh.

Gaia was having a good time. Meanwhile Sam was miserable in every way possible. He felt guilty. Tired. Jealous. Foolish. You name it. If it was bad, he felt it.

Sam leaned back against a brick wall and tried to

keep his head down. He didn't have a hat, or a big trench coat, or even sunglasses to make him harder to recognize. If Gaia looked out the window and saw Sam looking back, it would be the perfect end to a perfect day.

The radio buzzed in his pocket. Sam hated the sound. First thing in the morning these suckers were going back to the store. He dragged out the radio and squeezed the trigger.

"What do you want? *Over.*"

"A report," Ed replied. "You haven't even told me if you found her."

Sam said nothing.

"Sam?"

He smirked. "You didn't say '*over.*'" He sounded like a child. He didn't care.

"Over," Ed said.

"I found her," Sam replied. "She's okay. They're eating."

"Where?"

"Jimmy's Burrito."

Gaia laughed again. Another slice to the heart.

"Jimmy's?" Ed laughed. "Man, he got off cheap."

Sam glanced across the street and saw that Gaia was washing down a bite of something with her drink. He also saw that at least two people were giving him odd looks.

Sam turned his back to them. "Ed, I have to get off," he said.

"I need more details," Ed replied. "Booth or table?"

"Booth," Sam said through clenched teeth. He braced his free hand against the wall. "I'll talk to you later."

"Same side or across from each other?"

Sam rolled his eyes. "Across from each other."

"What are they eating?"

"Ed!" Sam shouted into the radio. "I can't tell what they're eating, and I don't read lips, so don't bother to ask what they're talking about. I'll call you if anything happens."

He snapped off the radio before Ed had a chance to reply and shoved it back into his coat pocket. His fingers brushed against the little box. Sam took it out. It didn't look like much.

Sam took a glance at Gaia, then tore at the paper on the outside of the box. Whoever had wrapped it had used plenty of tape. It took him a lot of tugging and tearing to get the paper unraveled. Once the paper was crumpled in his pocket, he was left with a featureless box of gray cardboard. He snapped a couple more pieces of tape and lifted off the lid.

The first thing Sam saw inside was a piece of folded paper. At the top of it was written *Sam Moon*. He picked it up, unfolded it, and started to read.

Sam—

I know that you have some connection with Gaia Moore. I hope that you continue to feel affection for her and that you will take the concerns expressed in this letter seriously.

Gaia is in danger. If I could take direct action to save her, I would, but circumstances prevent my appearance.

Instead I am passing this information along to you in hopes that you will know what to do with it. Watch out for Gaia. She is stronger than she appears to be, but she is not as strong as she believes. She can be hurt.

She needs you, Sam. Don't let her down.

Don't reveal the existence of this package or note to Gaia. For her own safety there are things she cannot know.

By the time he was done reading, Sam's heart was pounding in his ears. He read through the note again, clutching the page. There was no signature, no clue as to who had sent the package.

This little scrap of typing paper was about the weirdest thing Sam had ever run into in his life. Sure, he had been standing on the street playing undercover cop, but this note was straight out of some spy novel.

His immediate suspicion was that Ed had sent the package. Who else could have known that he was involved in any way with Gaia? It had to be a joke. If he called Ed on the radio, Sam could probably get Ed to confess.

But the longer he stood there, the less Sam believed in his own theory. Certain words in the note kept drumming against his brain.

Gaia is in danger.
She can be hurt.
She needs you, Sam.

He folded the note and shoved it back into his jacket pocket. Then Sam looked inside the little box again. There was another folded sheet of paper. `With shaking hands` Sam pulled it out and found that it was some kind of information form. Name. Age. That sort of thing.

Only this form had been attacked by someone with a big, fat black marker. Whole lines of the form were `completely blacked out,` but Sam could still read a few things.

`Eyes: Blue`

Several lines below that was another clear line.

`IQ: 146`

So whoever this sheet belonged to, they had blue eyes and they were smart. Sam wondered for a second if the sheet was about Gaia, but then he spotted another piece of uncovered info.

`Height: 6' 2"`

Gaia was tall for a girl, but not anywhere close to that tall.

The biggest area of readable type was a box of text marked `Evaluation.`

`Subject demonstrates almost complete lack of empathetic response. Does not act under social`

constraints. Does not operate in a frame of be-
havioral mores. It is our opinion that this subject should be considered deeply sociopathic.
Extreme caution is recommended.

Sam glanced back up at the glowing windows of
the restaurant. What did any of this have to do with
Gaia?

Sam put away the sheet. All that remained in the
box was a small black-and-white photo. Sam pulled it
out and raised it closer to his eyes.

Sunset was coming on fast, and the street-
lights were just beginning to flicker. In the gloom Sam
had to squint to make out the grainy, low-quality photo.

The guy in the photo was young. He had short, wavy
black hair and a squared-off chin. There was a flat, angry
expression on his face. He seemed a little familiar. Sam
knew that he had seen the guy in the photo before.

Then he remembered where.

Sam let the box fall out of his fingers and ran right
through the traffic on Thompson. He drew a chorus
of horn blasts as he darted between the cars, and a
couple of people had to slam on their brakes. Sam
didn't care. He charged up the steps into Jimmy's,
shoving people out of the way as he went.

But when Sam got inside, the booth at the side of
the restaurant was empty. Gaia was gone.

His eyes
narrowed, and
his teeth
clenched
together so
hard, Gaia
could see the
muscles bulge
at the corner
of his jaw.

**double
dare**

David

"WHAT TIME ARE THEY CLOSING the park?" David asked.

"I heard they were closing it at seven," Gaia responded. "Both the killings happened sometime around eleven or twelve. They probably want to make sure they get everybody out well ahead of that."

She took a deep breath and watched the fog it caused disappear into the night sky.

"Let's go," David said.

Gaia looked at him. There was no way to know what he was thinking. His expression conveyed nothing.

"It's almost seven," Gaia said. "The police probably won't let us in." Not that that mattered to her.

"Are you scared?" David asked.

A challenge. Interesting. Gaia felt the skin around her eyes draw tight.

"I'm not scared," she said.

"Then let's go." David pointed. "If they have the gates blocked, we can always sneak over the fence."

Gaia stopped, hands in pockets. She looked him directly in the eyes, giving him a chance to back out. "If we go into the park, we'll probably get caught."

"So?" He kept walking. She followed.

"So, they'll put us in jail," she said. "Aren't you scared of that?"

"No." He turned to look at her, walking backward. "I guess I'm just naturally fearless."

"WHAT DID YOU SAY?"

Gaia stumbled to a stop on the sidewalk and leaned against the iron fence that guarded the park's south side.

Two Davids

David shrugged. "I said I was naturally fearless." He struck a dramatic pose, chin lifted, chest out, eyebrows lowered. "Intrepid explorer David Twain, ready and able to penetrate the deepest mysteries of unexplored regions."

Coincidence. That's all it was. It wasn't like *fearless* was a word reserved just for her. "You really aren't scared to go in the park?"

"Not me," he said. He folded his arms over his still puffed-out chest and raised an eyebrow. "What about you, little lady?" he said with a Hollywood cowboy accent. "You a-feared to go in that thar patch of woods?"

There was something odd going on here. Something had shifted.

This seemed like the same funny, talkative guy Gaia had shared burritos with back at Jimmy's. Obviously it was the same David. Only now it seemed like there was somebody else there, too. Like there were two completely different people looking at her with those dark blue eyes.

"All right," Gaia said, refusing to tear her gaze from his. "Let's go."

"Cool," David said. He stood up on the tips of his toes and looked over her head. "But there's already a cop down by the entrance. You're probably right that they won't let us by."

Gaia looked up at the fence. "So I guess we'll have to go in this way."

She braced herself, bent low, and jumped. Gaia's beat-up right knee protested, but she still managed to grab the top of the fence. A few seconds later she was over and in the bushes on the other side.

David clapped in rapid applause. "I think you're doing the wrong thing by staying in school," he said through the fence. "You should definitely run off and join the circus."

"I'll think about it," Gaia replied. "Are you coming over here, or are you too much of a chicken?"

There was nothing funny about David's reply this time. His eyes narrowed, and his teeth clenched together so hard, Gaia could see the muscles bulge at the corner of his jaw. He wasn't happy.

He jumped for the fence. With his longer arms he had no trouble grabbing the iron crossbar at the top. It took him a little longer to pull himself up, and he wasn't nearly as smooth working his way over the top, but less than thirty seconds later he dropped to the ground beside Gaia.

"I told you," he said. "I'm fearless."

Gaia started to wonder if maybe he was telling the truth.

"WHERE'S THE SPOT?"

"This way," Gaia replied. She circled a small fountain and pushed south past the makeshift stage where bands sometimes played on the weekends. She was moving fast. She wanted to get there and get it over with. "Why do you want to see it, anyway? You're not some kind of murder groupie, are you?"

David laughed. A normal laugh. "No. Absolutely not. I just wanted you to know I wasn't afraid."

"You keep saying that." She looked toward him, then back at the path, her ponytail of golden hair flipping back and forth as she moved. "Why are you so worried about not being afraid?"

David took a couple of quick steps and moved up to walk beside her. "I just think it would be cool, that's all. Not to be afraid of anything."

"Why?"

"Because then you'd really be free, wouldn't you?"

Gaia blinked. Interesting theory.

They passed under a group of oaks, and the shadows thickened around them. "Being fearless wouldn't make a person happy."

David reached up and snapped off a small dead limb. "Why not?" he said. "It's being afraid of things that makes people sad."

Gaia shook her head. "That's not true. Even without fear you still get lonely, or angry, or depressed."

"There's nothing wrong with angry," David said. "Sometimes you have to be angry. Sometimes it's what you need."

Gaia couldn't argue with that. "And what about the others?"

"What? Sad and lonely?" David shrugged. "I don't really feel those things."

Gaia reached the edge of a concrete path and stopped. "It doesn't sound like you feel much."

"All I need."

For a moment the two of them stood in silence, then Gaia turned her back on him, raised a hand, and pointed at the open space on the other side of the path.

189

"This is it," she said. "This is where they found the bodies." She turned back to look at David. She met his gaze dead-on. "But I think you already knew that."

DAVID REACHED BEHIND HIS BACK and pulled out a long knife. The blue-steel blade was almost black in the dim light, but the sharp edge caught the glow from distant  streetlamps and threw off glittering sparks.

Damn, he loved that.

"You're smarter than I anticipated," he said. "I like it." He stretched out a hand to Gaia. "Come on, I'll make it painless."

"No, you won't," Gaia said.

David grinned. "You're right. This is going to hurt like hell."

There was a
wildness in
his eyes. **the**

gentleman

How had she
not noticed
it before?

"I'M NOT THE ONE WHO LET HER
get away," Ed's voice
crackled through the
radio.

The Rescue Party

Sam glared at the lit-
tle yellow transistor. "I
was distracted," he said.
"Besides, it doesn't mat-
ter now. We've got to find a way into the park."

"I'm with you on that," Ed replied. "So, what's the plan?"

Sam looked across the street. There were now two policemen standing by the nearest entrance to the park, and he didn't think for a moment that the officers were just going to step aside and let them in.

"I'm going to have to go over the fence," Sam said after a few seconds' thought. "I don't see any other way."

"What about me?" asked Ed. "I don't know if you've noticed, but I'm not very good at going over things."

The thought had already occurred to Sam, but he didn't have a solution. "I need your help so I can get in. You come down here and distract the police."

Ed sighed. "That's me. Ed Fargo, distraction specialist."

"What?" Sam asked, confused.

"Forget it," Ed answered. "Distract them how?"

Sam glanced around and winced. Every second counted. There was no time to argue. "I don't know. Ask directions. Fake a heart attack. Just get them looking the wrong way long enough for me to climb the fence."

He didn't wait for Ed's reply. Instead he switched off the radio and dropped it into his pocket. He darted across the intersection, took a last longing look at the gate, then walked quickly toward the corner where the police would be far away and nearly out of sight.

Sam was only halfway to the corner when he got a break. The sounds of yelling and of running feet came from the direction of the entrance. Sam turned and saw the policemen wrestling a man with a potbelly and a stiff, graying beard.

It was the best chance Sam was going to get. There was no point in waiting for Ed when there was already a perfect distraction. He hurried across the sidewalk, bent low, then jumped for the top of the fence. His fingers managed to catch the square bar at the top, but the metal bit painfully into his palms. He started to bleed. Gritting his teeth, he slowly pulled, kicked, and scrambled his way to the top.

He stopped there for a second to catch his

breath. Down at the entrance the police were busy putting handcuffs on the bearded man. No one was looking.

Sam smiled. He had made it. Now he only had to find Gaia before it was too late.

He started to jump, but his foot slipped and his jump turned into a fall. The cuff of his pants caught on one of the points at the top of the fence. Sam pendulumed back and smashed against the fence with bone-jarring force. He kicked his feet, but the thin strip of fabric held him in place as firmly as a rope. He grabbed at the bars and tried to pull himself back up.

A hand grabbed Sam by the collar and jerked him away from the fence. Upside down, he found himself staring into a stern face topped with iron gray hair and an NYPD cap.

"What do you think you're doing, son?"

"I've got to get into the park," said Sam. "There's this girl, and she's in danger."

"Really?" The policeman grabbed Sam's arms and pulled them roughly behind his back. A moment later Sam felt hard, cold steel close around his wrists.

"What are you doing?" Sam shouted.

"My job," said the policeman. "What's your name?"

"Sam . . . Sam Moon."

"Well, Sam Moon, you're under arrest."

GAIA ALMOST LAUGHED.

You Die

She'd always thought she had perfect bad-guy radar. How wrong she was.

"What are we going to do now?" she said. There was a wildness in his eyes. How had she not noticed it before?

He looked at Gaia as if she were completely brain-dead. "Oh, please!" He pointed his nose up in the air and put on a thick British accent. "That should be immediately obvious to the most casual observer." Then he looked her directly in the eyes. "You die."

He was about to lunge. But Gaia wasn't going to take on a knife. "What's the matter? Scared to fight me hand to hand?"

David paused. He looked at the knife. His knuckles turned white. "I fear nothing from you," he said. He placed his weapon on the ground.

Gaia had to struggle to watch him and not look at the knife. Watch the opponent's every move. Every twitch. It was a basic rule of fighting, something her father had told her a thousand times.

But she couldn't stop herself. She checked the position of the knife. And that's when David hit her.

Gaia had been hit before. You didn't make it through the belts in any martial art without having your ass handed to you a hundred times. Gaia's nose had been bloodied by the best. But she was sure she had never been hit harder than that first blow from David.

He hit her with a `straight left` that knocked Gaia all the way across the path. She snapped through the stupid plastic police tape at the edge of the field, slipped on the grass, and fell.

Judo saved her life. To the naked eye, judo seems to be all about grabbing people by the arm and flipping them in the air. That wasn't it at all. `Judo was about falling.`

Gaia was falling backward. If she fought against that kind of fall, she would only spin her arms in the air and still end up sitting on the grass. Instead Gaia went with it. She pushed off hard, threw back her hands, and took the fall, using her arms as `shock absorbers`. Another quick push and Gaia was back on her feet.

David was almost on top of her. He swung again, but this time Gaia caught his wrist and pulled it past her.

For a moment they were almost face-to-face—so close, all Gaia had to do was move her lips to end her long kissing drought. The thought turned her stomach.

David pulled left, then quickly back to the right. It was an elementary move, and Gaia was braced for it, but David was very strong. Gaia was great at keeping her balance, but not even she could keep her balance when both of her feet were off the ground. That wasn't a rule of judo—that was a rule of gravity.

She didn't go down, but it was close. Before Gaia could recover, David drove a pile-driver fist into her side so hard, Gaia imagined she could hear her ribs crack. Maybe it wasn't imagination.

David grabbed at Gaia. He took her arm, jerked her back toward him, and threw another punch. Gaia blocked with a forearm and drove a knee into his gut at the same time.

David released his grip on her and fell back a step. Gaia didn't let him.

She took a quick step forward and delivered a kick that took David across the hip. Another that struck him in the thigh. He staggered and stepped back again.

This was more like it. Gaia spun, trying to deliver a solid kick to the body.

David blocked it easily. He took the blow against the flat of one palm, pushed sharply to throw Gaia off balance, then followed the push with a straight left that took her right between the eyes.

This punch was even harder than the first. The sound of his knuckles hitting her skull was amazing. It was like somebody had broken a rock with a sledgehammer. Like an ax biting into a tree.

Sparks of red light swarmed through Gaia's eyes. Her ears started to ring. All at once her arms and legs gained fifty pounds each.

She tried to get her hands up to block, but they didn't listen to orders. Another punch whistled in and hit her on the temple. This one was a right hook. That was another thing Gaia had learned early about fighting: If you're going to get hit in the face, get hit by a straight punch. Straight punches hurt, but if you get hit from the side, hurt doesn't even come close.

The night flashed into bright shades of yellow and blue. There was a sound in Gaia's ears like the roar from a hundred seashells.

She backpedaled fast and managed to avoid the next shot. Another punch came. Blocked. Another. Dodged. Another. It glanced off the top of her head without shooting any fireworks through her skull, but this time she felt the warm flow of blood across her forehead.

Gaia kicked out wildly and was lucky to hit David in the side. She didn't think it really hurt him, but at least it made him back off.

"Getting scared yet?" David taunted.

Somehow David knew about her, but this wasn't the time to figure out how.

Gaia didn't waste breath on talking. Her head was starting to clear, but the blood from her forehead was dripping into her eyes. Gaia's ribs ached, and the knee she had messed up the night before was starting to get in on the complaints. If she was going to end this on her feet, Gaia had to end it soon.

David launched another punch, but it was a long overhand right, and Gaia had time to get out of the way. She feinted a punch with her left, ducked his response, and stepped back. Did the same thing with the right and took another backward step.

There was a rhythm to David's fighting. If Gaia could work it out, she could time her shots and plaster him without taking blows of her own. All she needed was time.

Suddenly David lunged forward and grabbed Gaia with both his arms. Grabbing like that was a really stupid move—unless you were as strong as a gorilla. David could have made gorillas beg for mercy.

He squeezed the breath out of Gaia in a painful rush, and this time she knew the cracking sound had to be at least one of her ribs turning into a two-piece. She kicked her feet along David's shins, but he didn't let her free. So Gaia lowered her head and butted him in the face.

David howled. His nose exploded in blood. He lost his hold on Gaia and clamped a hand over his face.

Gaia drew a painful breath and jumped forward. She got off a kick to the chest, and David was staggering.

Then a kick to his side, and he groaned. His hand came away from his face. Blood spilled over his lips and dripped from the point of his chin. In seconds his shirt was stained by a spreading pool of darkness.

He punched. Gaia blocked and counterpunched. It wasn't a perfect hit on his solar plexus, but it was good enough to make David gasp for air. She hit him again, driving her fist into his gut so deep, Gaia wouldn't have been surprised to feel his backbone.

David made a wild, flailing punch. Gaia blocked it easily. He threw another, and she turned it aside. He stepped back. He was breathing hard, and Gaia could hear air whistling through his smashed nose.

"What about you?" she said. "Still fearless?"

"I ... don't ... have ... anything to fear from you," he said.

It was time to end this thing. Gaia started forward, planning to put her foot where David's face was, but something grabbed her by the ankles. She glanced down. Tape. Stupid yellow police tape. Somehow yards of it had become tangled around her legs. It snapped easily enough, but it distracted Gaia for a second.

A second was too much to give up in the middle of a fight.

When she looked up, David's fist was six inches from her face and coming in fast. Gaia tried to dodge, but the blow still caught her on her right jawbone.

This time Gaia didn't just see sparks. This time she went someplace. Someplace where squirrels played banjos and the trees were cotton-candy pink. The seashells were roaring again, and this time they were joined by a brass band. Gaia tried to put out her hands and catch herself, but for a second there she couldn't even tell if she had hands. Gaia didn't know if she was standing or lying on the ground.

She wasn't even sure if she was still alive.

It took a few seconds for the furry-tailed rats to put away their instruments and the night to go back to something like normal. When it did, Gaia figured out that she was on the ground. There was something under her hands. Grass, but something else, too. Something gritty and crumbly. It took her a moment to realize that it was chalk—the chalk that had marked the body lines of the dead girls.

From somewhere behind her Gaia heard David laugh. "That's great," he said. "That's perfect. I'll go get the knife. You just stay put." His smashed nose turned "that's" into "dat's" and "great" into "gweat." It would have been funny if he wasn't about to kill her.

Gaia struggled to sit up, but the best she could manage was to roll onto one knee. The banjos might be packed away, but her head was still spinning. Everything hurt.

David didn't seem to be in much better shape. He limped as he crossed the field and stopped near the path for a moment to lean against a tree. He was banged up pretty good, but he was still going to kill Gaia. He knelt down beside the path and reached for the knife.

Gaia saw salvation coming from twenty feet away. David saw it, too, but he was slow. He barely managed to turn his head before Ed Fargo hit him like a freight train.

David was coming. He was climbing along Gaia's body, and he still had his knife.

a time to die

GAIA WOULD HAVE SCREAMED FOR

Ground Rule Double

Ed to stop if she'd had the time. The collision happened with such speed that it looked more like a car accident than a wheelchair ramming.

One of David's hands, the one reaching for the knife, was trapped under a wheel. Instantly every finger on that hand had snapped, one after another, like twigs. The metal frame of the chair caught him under the arm, rolled him over, and left him sprawling on the ground. His head hit the asphalt with a sickening crack, and Gaia saw every limb of his body go slack.

David was down for the count.

At the moment of impact Ed was thrown up and out. He flew almost twenty feet in a low arc before he thumped to the ground between a pair of pines. Freed of his weight, the chair rolled on another few paces, curved, then toppled on its side.

That was when Gaia hit the ground. The paralyzation had set in.

For the space of five seconds everything was still and quiet. Then the broken bodies started to move.

David was up first. Gaia couldn't believe her eyes.

She'd thought he was done. Unconscious. Useless. Yet he climbed to his feet, clutching his broken, bleeding hand against his chest. Who *was* this guy?

"Gonna . . . kill . . . you both," he grunted. He looked in the grass, located the knife, and lifted it in his good hand.

Gaia struggled to rise. She had to stop him.

She couldn't move. Gaia's muscles twitched and squirmed like bags full of snakes, and she was barely able to raise her head from the ground.

David looked at her, then looked at Ed. Slowly his split lips widened into a horrible, bloody grin.

"Which one first?" he said.

Me, thought Gaia. Come for me. But even her mouth had shut down. She could do nothing but watch as David decided who would die.

A Hundred Feet Away

EVERY BRANCH GRABBED AT HIS coat. Every stone seemed to be out to trip his feet.

Tom Moore ran desperately through the woods. Loki wasn't the only one with fake identification, but it had taken Tom much longer than he expected to convince the police guarding the park that he should be allowed inside.

He pulled the gun from his coat pocket as he ran and thumbed off the safety. He only hoped it wasn't too late.

GAIA OPENED HER HAND AND CLOSED

it again. It wasn't much, but it was something. Her body was returning to her.

The Last Reserves

A dozen yards away, David limped toward the pilot of the overturned wheelchair. Ed had his hands under him and was dragging himself back as fast as he could. It wasn't fast enough. David would be on him in seconds.

Ed was about to die.

Gaia reached down and pulled at her reserves of strength. The tank was almost empty. She absently thought of what her father used to say when he had driven the family car long past the point the needle dropped to *E*.

Vapors. I'm running on vapors.

Slowly she rolled over onto her trembling arms.

Painfully she pushed her aching legs under her and climbed to her feet.

David glanced at her, then continued after Ed.

Gaia tried to go toward them, but she could barely manage a step. Her head swam, and her knees were weak. She wasn't going to be fast enough. There was only ten feet between David and Ed. There was at least thirty feet between Gaia and David. There was no way for Gaia to get to Ed in time.

"Hey," she called in a hoarse whisper.

David kept after Ed.

"Wasn't I the one you wanted?" Gaia's voice was a little stronger this time.

The gap between David and Ed was down to five feet. David raised his knife to strike.

"Hey, chicken!" Gaia screamed.

David froze.

"Are you afraid to fight me?"

David pivoted like a rusty screen door and looked at Gaia. "I'm not afraid of you."

"Then show me."

Gaia had trained herself to hold back. Even when she was fighting a mugger or a thief, she was careful to stop, not injure. She threw those rules away.

David staggered toward her with the knife held high. He pointed the glittering blade toward Gaia's face and swung the edge from side to side.

David was strong. David was fast. But by now Gaia

knew one thing for sure—David wasn't well trained. She leaned back her arm as if she were going to throw a punch.

That was all it took to draw David's attention. He leaped at her with surprising speed.

Gaia fell back. Her balance was gone. She was going to hit the ground—there was no stopping that—but there was enough strength in her legs for one last good kick. She pivoted on her left foot, kicking and falling at the same time.

David's right leg broke with a noise like a gunshot. A thin, high whine escaped his blood-smeared mouth as both he and Gaia toppled to the ground.

GAIA LAY ON HER BACK IN THE

grass, biding her time. She knew David thought she was spent. Done. Gone. But she was just waiting. Overhead, the gloomy clouds that had covered the sky all day finally parted. Stars peeked through.

Seeing Stars

She'd never seen stars in the city. But they were up there now, sparkling down at Gaia as if they had come out just to watch the bitter end.

From somewhere nearby she could hear sounds of breathing. They weren't pleasant sounds. The breathing was kind of wet, as if the person making the noise was pulling as much blood as air into his lungs with every breath.

A hand grasped Gaia's ankle. Another closed on her knee. Something hard and cold pressed against the skin of her leg.

David was coming. He was climbing along Gaia's body, and he still had his knife.

Patience. Patience.

One of David's hands came down in the middle of Gaia's stomach with painful force. The other hand, the hand with the knife, slid along her arm.

It was strange. After a lifetime of feeling alone, or embarrassed, or just plain angry, what Gaia felt now was calm. She had done everything she could. Somewhere, way down in her brain, a voice was calling for her to get up. Get up and fight. But that voice was faint and far away.

Gaia was tired. Very, very tired. But maybe, just maybe, if she waited until just the right moment, she could finish this thing. And maybe she could live through it.

Tangled black hair came into view. Even from this close, Gaia could barely recognize the face as David's. His nose flattened like a pancake. His face painted over in blood. His lips pulled back in a snarl of rage.

Slowly David dragged himself beside Gaia. Then he raised the knife and held it above her chest.

"See?" he croaked through bloody lips. "See, I'm the best after all. I can beat you. I'm the best."

Gaia had no idea what he was talking about. David sat up straighter, raised the knife high, and plunged it down at Gaia. She raised her arms. Watched his eyes widen in surprise. And then it happened.

THE SOUND CAME THREE TIMES, all very close together. Hiss. Hiss. Hiss. It was like the noise of air being let out of a bicycle tire. Like water falling on a hot skillet. **Popped**

DAVID'S SHOULDER ERUPTED. HIS body twitched around to the left, and blood poured out across his chest. There was a cracking, and **Splatter** for a moment Gaia saw something white exposed in the core of his wounds.

Bone.

"I . . . ," said David. "You . . ." A bloody foam spilled from his lips. It hit her face with a sickening splatter. David toppled off of Gaia and fell still at her side.

For several seconds Gaia lay there, trying to understand what had happened. Something had hurt David. Something had stopped him.

She wasn't going to die. Not now. It seemed like an impossible thought.

Someone stepped into view at the edge of the clearing. Gaia turned her head for a better look.

She saw a tall figure in a trench coat. She saw the gun in his hand. She knew the face. Her uncle. Apparently he couldn't call or write, but he had an uncanny ability to materialize when she was in danger.

The figure at the edge of the clearing only stood there for a few moments. Then he turned and stepped back into the shadows of the trees.

Gaia closed her eyes.

IT TOOK ED NEARLY TEN MINUTES TO

Exit, Stage Left

get his wheelchair upright, get his battered self into it, and roll across the damp ground to Gaia's side. For every one of those ten minutes he harbored the unthinkable thought that she was dead.

And yet when he actually reached the center of the clearing, he was amazed to see Gaia sit up and push her ratty hair away from her face.

Total, utter, complete, euphoric relief.

Ed calmed his heaving chest before he let himself open his mouth. "Hey, Gaia," he called. "Your new boyfriend's the killer."

Gaia made a tired, gasping noise that might have been laughter on the planet Exhaustion. She stood slowly, swayed on her feet for a few seconds, then staggered over to lean against Ed's chair.

"Thanks for the update," she said. "How did you get in here?"

"Easy." Ed rapped his knuckles against the armrest of the wheelchair. "I got in while Sam was getting arrested."

Gaia blinked. "Sam got arrested?"

"Worked out great as a distraction," Ed said with a grin.

"Okay," said Gaia. She shook her head and swayed so badly that she almost lost her grip on the chair.

"What happened?" asked Ed. "I couldn't see what was going on. I was so afraid. . . . I mean, I was afraid he was going to . . ."

"Kill me?" Gaia nodded slowly. "He almost did. We'll leave him for the police."

David suddenly moaned. His broken, bleeding hand scrabbled at the grass.

Gaia pulled back her foot and kicked him again. The moaning stopped.

Ed looked at her and shook his head. "You know, sometimes I can't tell if you're really brave or just perpetually pissed off."

TOM KNEW HE HAD TO GET MOVING.

Broken

Once Loki and his operatives had figured out that Tom Moore was here, they wouldn't pass up the chance to bag him when they had it.

He turned to leave and heard movement behind him. Quickly he pressed himself against the dark trunk of an elm and waited.

A man was coming across the field. It was a tall man, a man Tom had no trouble recognizing.

Loki walked straight across the trampled field. He paused a moment beside the broken form on the ground. Then he knelt, grabbed the boy by the hair, and delivered a sharp slap across the face.

David groaned.

"Wake up," said Loki. Another slap. "Open your eyes."

The eyelids fluttered.

"She shot you?" Loki said. "She used a gun?"

The boy on the ground said something. From his place by the trees, Tom couldn't hear the words, but he could hear Loki's reply.

"Home?" Loki shook his head. "I'm afraid that boat has already sailed. You're worthless to me now."

The boy spoke again, and this time Tom could make out his words.

"I'll tell," he said. His voice was high and raw, like a child who had been crying. "I'll tell them everything."

"Yes." Loki released his grip on the boy's blood-soaked hair and stood. "Yes, I'm sure you would."

Tom knew what was coming next. He turned away from the scene and started to make his way through the woods. He had gone no more than a dozen steps before he heard the gunshot.